The Innkeeper's House
A Hickory Grove Novel

Elizabeth Bromke

THE INNKEEPER'S HOUSE

PUBLISHING IN THE PINES

White Mountains, Arizona

For my readers.

Chapter 1—Greta

Four cardboard boxes, two large plastic storage bins, and a bucket with cleaning supplies stood in an orderly line on her classroom floor. Greta Houston pushed her fingertips into her temples and rubbed in circles.

Inadvertently, a blonde wisp of her hair got pinched under her finger. "*Ouch*," she whispered when it snapped out of her scalp. After rubbing the tender spot, she raked her fingers through her short waves and tied them into a messy ponytail at the back of her head. Strands fell away along her hairline, and she blew them out of her face and sighed with a finalizing huff. "It's for the best," Greta declared triumphantly to herself, striding to her desk to begin the emptying process.

It *was* for the best.

She'd made do at Innovative Learning Academy, the only place with an open teaching position mid school year. At least, the only one in the ten-mile radius of Mile Square, where Kadan both lived and worked. She'd had to settle in order to live near her *ex*-fiancé.

Instead of high school sophomores with their classic literature and compelling research papers, she'd accepted stinky fourth graders with their mind-numbing spelling bees and cliché science projects. Instead of a classroom with windows, she'd been relegated to a pod on the inside of the school building. After all, without the proper elementary certification, Greta was little more than a warm body, holding a place for the pregnant teacher on leave.

Greta's career wasn't the only part of her life in which she'd been forced to make concessions. Oh, no. When she met Kadan, she figured that his money (and he had a lot of it) would equate to some sort of upper-middle-class utopia. After all, he'd promised that if she bought the first-floor condo just two miles from his office, he would help cover the mortgage until they were married. At that point, they could turn it into rental income. It could be her little weekend project after they built the perfect family home.

In her mind's eye, together, Greta and Kadan would move mountains out in green-lawned suburbia with exactly two-point-five children and a minivan. She would tend a modest vegetable garden and plant flowers while the kids played in a safely fenced yard. Every weekday morning all three-point-five of them would wave pleasantly to Kadan as he left for work, his suit and tie in perfect order, for a pat eight-hour workday. Family dinners would commence at precisely five o'clock, leaving plenty of evening for Mommy and Daddy to cuddle on the sofa as the children snoozed upstairs.

As the thirty-something ought to have realized much sooner in life, reality never jibed with one's fantasy. The woulds quickly became would-nots.

Besides the prevailing issue of her disappointing teaching position and oversized mortgage payment on a condo with no yard to speak of, other issues cropped up, multiplying in a short time span. Just weeks after he proposed, Kadan's promises wore thin. That, and Greta started to learn about his lifestyle more intimately than she had when they were only dating on the weekends.

Soon enough, Greta learned that he was happy to keep his sports car. He might only want *one* child. "*Down the road,*" he'd said. He was allergic to grass, by the way. And, in fact, Kadan's days were quite long. Not as long as their engagement promised to be, however. She wanted two months. He wanted two years. Two *years*! Who could *wait* two years? Her clock was ticking, but the only thing pressuring Kadan was a sense of obligation, and traditionally, a three-year courtship was *appropriate*. She started to hate the word. By the bitter end, it became clear that a former country bumpkin like Greta Houston had no say in a relationship with a big-city heir. And, she had no place in his high-falutin' life.

And yet, it was *not* Greta who called the whole thing off.

***

Initially, in the throes of her breakup, Greta assumed she'd be stuck there, in Indianapolis. Surely, she could find a better teaching job. But after turning to her older brother, Rhett, a plan materialized for her.

Always the hero type, he'd flown into action, connecting with his so-called friend, Maggie. Greta remembered Maggie from her childhood. She was older, Rhett's age. A little wild. A lot beautiful. Maggie, to Greta, was an enigmatic figure, cooler and more popular. A cheerleader type except more personable and friendly. At least, to Greta she had been.

It turned out that Maggie had just moved into her family's old farm. With Rhett's help, she was converting the barn into a little apartment. Greta suspected there was more to that story, but she didn't have the energy to badger her big brother. Instead, she'd weakly agreed to his idea: list her condo, quit her sub gig, and move home. To Hickory Grove.

It would do her good to lay low for a while. Even if she only spent a month there, Greta could apply for a teaching position in Louisville or Corydon. Maybe she would reach out to some of her old classmates from college, the friends who'd faded away over the years. All she needed was a temporary fix. Then, she could leave heartbreak in her past, never to look back again.

After all, nothing would keep Greta in the rural farming town. Not her brother. Or a cute barn. Not the ragamuffin children who lived at the farmhouse. Not even the bittersweet memories of growing up among the green hills and fireflies. The fish frys and sweet tea. *Nothing*.

Chapter 2—Luke

Luke Hart freed his lanyard from beneath a crisp white t-shirt and drew the silver whistle to his mouth. Three sharp bursts trilled from his lips.

The sound echoed across the baseball field behind Hickory Grove Junior High, where a moving blob of unathletic preteens whined beneath the warm June sun. Their shoulders slumped forward, none opted to hustle. Instead, they muttered under their breath and strolled slower than molasses over to the chain link fence. Wind sprints were more wind and less sprint when it came to summer school.

Luke shook his head and grinned.

"Pop quiz!" he shouted at the small group of flunkies. "Why did Cinderella get kicked out of the baseball game?"

Some of them shielded their eyes from the sun, half curious. The rest kicked at the ground, blowing up puffs of dirt across the bright green outfield.

When no one replied, he answered it himself, holding back his own laughter. "Because she kept running away from the ball!"

Several moans gave way to restrained chuckles. The social requirements of junior high prevented the poor fools from revealing just how little they minded spending their summer vacation outside with him. Still, Luke saw the hint of joy in their eyes and in their awkward attempts to pretend they were too cool for a phys. ed. joke.

Summer school P.E. was a special kind of experience. Typically, the types of kids who had to make up a math class or retake science were naturally less motivated. At the far-left end of the bell curve? Sure, but they were still *on* the curve.

Then you had your P.E. summer school kids. They were a different breed altogether. The sort of thirteen-year-old boy who failed gym class was not the sort Luke could personally relate to. That was just the thing, though. Sure, Luke loved sports, but he didn't become a teacher or even a coach to train up the next Michael Jordan. He did it for the kids. Plain and simple.

Luke would have had his own kids by then if it wasn't for the fact that dating did not exist in Hickory Grove, Indiana. 'Less of course you didn't mind getting friendly with a distant cousin or one of your pal's ex-wives. Luke minded that sort of thing, though, much to his own chagrin. And he wasn't too interested in traveling to and from the big city just to bar hop. He'd rather tinker around in his shed or study tape for practice.

The move from Louisville, with all its hustle and bustle, to a starkly different rural community that drifted out west of the Ohio River was dramatic. All signs ought to have pointed Luke anywhere else in the world. Then again, he would not have stopped to consider that fact. Luke wasn't much of a planner. More of a go-along-to-get-alonger. And anyway, he *knew* the town from family visits. In fact, he only managed to nail a coaching and teaching gig with H.G.U.S.D. because of his Hart Family connections. That's right. Some may think that education would be the one professional world distinctly devoid of nepotism. The opposite was true.

Once class ended, and Luke was free to go about his business, he settled into his office, a small square space inside of the boys' locker room. With little to do during June and July, teaching summer school was a no brainer. He could make some extra cash to stow away for a rainy day and get ready for the upcoming football season in one fell swoop.

Luke tugged open the top drawer in his metal desk and withdrew his phone before tapping out a quick message.

Lunch? Mally's?

Mark Ketchum taught Social Studies at Hickory Grove J.H.S. and had signed on for summer school, too. He was also the head coach of the high school football team and Luke's superior in that capacity. Though their age gap was significant, the two had hit it off easily, meeting up for Wing Wednesdays and spending their Sundays together throughout football season. *After* mass, of course. There was a loose commonality there, too. Mark, a former Deacon, spent his whole life in the Catholic Church. Currently, though, he didn't practice and instead identified as a term he was convinced he'd coined: Casual Catholic. Luke didn't mind. He wasn't the type to pass judgment on how other people lived their lives. What mattered about a person in Luke's eyes was his heart. Not his parish record.

Meet you there. Maybe they hired a girlfriend for you. Maybe one for me, too. LOL.

Luke cringed at Mark's teasing. Would he love to meet a local girl and fall in love? Sure. Was it going to happen? Suffice it to say that Luke started considering his aunt's plea that he look into Saint Meinrad's Monastery. Still, the two men's singleness was another dollop of glue that bound them. Mark was simply antsier about it than his younger counterpart.

***

"Chicken tenders and fries, please." Luke smiled at the girl taking his order. Gretchen Engel. He'd had her in class just a few years back.

She nodded and smiled in return. "A Pepsi, too, Coach Hart?"

He shook his head. "Just a water. Thanks, Gretchen."

She took Mark's order then scurried off to the kitchen.

Mark adjusted his silverware into a neat cascade and unfolded his napkin on his lap. "So, how is June?"

It was a touchy subject, though. A grimace stretched Luke's mouth. "I'm going to head to the hospital later." He kept his eyes on his napkin, folding it as many times as it would go, into a thick, papery wedge. June Hart took a fall a week before. Turned out to be a blood clot, and she was still lying in a coma, machines breathing for her day and night. Luke didn't want to think about it. He'd gone every day, so far, to visit. And each time it got harder, not easier. In fact, he really did not want to visit her at all anymore. It might just kill him to see the old woman, her chest rising unnaturally. Her skin gray and slipping away from her skeleton.

Luke prayed for good news. He prayed for a phone call from his aunt. *She made it! I'm driving her home now!* He prayed the next time that he saw Mamaw Hart, that she'd be tucked beneath an afghan on her rocking chair in the little house behind the bed-and-breakfast she still owned. He prayed he'd get another chance to convince her to let him take over doing repairs so she didn't have to keep hiring out. He prayed for strength to be a better grandson and step up to the plate. He prayed for a miracle.

Mark cleared his throat and shifted on the bench. It squeaked. Luke glanced up and offered a grin.

"Can I do anything?" Mark asked, rearranging his silverware again.

Luke shook his head and changed the conversation as best he could. "Is your friend going to apply for the English position?"

Glancing up, Mark's face lifted. He, too, was happy to divert the topic. "Oh, no. He found a job up north."

"What do you think Mrs. Cook will do? Think she'll merge the classes?" Talking about school hires was about as bland a thing as one could talk about, and yet it drove many of Mark and Luke's breeze-shooting. There lay something of a hope each time another Hickory Grove Unified faculty member bit the dust. Who'd replace them? Who'd show up for the pre-service trainings?

Shrugging, Mark thanked the waitress as she dropped their drinks and meals. He took a generous bite of his burger then spoke through a full mouth. "What about your mom?"

Luke laughed. "She's retiring. She's had enough. Anyways, she doesn't teach English."

Besides the fact that he liked working with kids, Luke's folks had inspired him to go for teaching and turn it into the *family biz*, as his dad would say. His mom had been a school secretary but turned into a kindergarten teacher after some years. His father had served as Southern Community College's head football coach for nearly forty years. A legend. Luke's hero.

Kurt Hart, Luke's dad, was born and raised in Hickory Grove, the child of parents who adopted when they struggled to have babies of their own. Siblings Liesel and Kurt grew up and made their own ways in the world, Liesel returning to Hickory Grove after a failed attempt to join a convent, and Kurt fleeing to the big city with his high school sweetheart, May. The marriage turned sour, and the two split when Luke was still in school. It had crushed Kurt, though, and he never did recover. In fact, his health took such a hit that he suffered from a heart attack and passed years later.

It was Luke's Aunt Liesel who'd invited him to pursue a teaching opportunity in the tiny town just a thirty-minute drive from Louisville. Too traumatized to stick around Louisville, he took her up on it. Over time and after he'd purchased his own place near the school, Luke settled in enough, making new friends and returning home less and less. In fact, Hickory Grove became his home. There, he felt close to his roots but far enough away from the memory of his dad.

"Maybe you should take a trip down to UofL and *recruit*." Mark threw Luke a knowing wink, but Luke swatted it away.

Luke rolled his eyes. "I'm thirty-six, man. And I'm a *teacher*. And a coach. I'm not interested in college girls."

Mark sulked. "Sorry about that. I don't know what's the matter with me."

"Seems like you need to get out more." Luke gave his friend a pointed look and took a long swig from his water and stared out the window. Maybe he needed to get out more, too.

His phone buzzed on the table beside his plate and he glanced down at it. A call from his aunt. It could be about anything. It could be about the Fourth of July parade she was planning for Little Flock Catholic. It could be about her air conditioner making a funny noise.

But he knew in his gut it was way worse.

Chapter 3—Greta

On her drive into town, Greta had made no less than a dozen phone calls, pulling off to the side of the road each time she had to search for and dial a new number. She called the girls from her teaching cohort at UofL. She called a cousin whose number she learned from another cousin. She called three school districts in the greater Louisville area.

None of her personal contacts had any leads on openings for the fall. They each cooed over hearing from her and swore up and down to make a lunch date somewhere in the area. Maybe by then something would crop up and they'd be able to help.

The school secretaries rattled off website addresses where Greta might put in an application. However, she'd *better be warned* that they did *not anticipate any turnover for the new school year.*

The result of every single phone call was the same: a dead end.

She'd have to look outside of her comfort zone if she wanted to get a job teaching English. Maybe broaden her search to Chicago or Nashville. She might have to consider applying with the inner-city schools. That might be even better than a suburban placement. She might make a *real* difference in a lower-income district.

All Greta needed was an interview, and she'd take whatever came first. After that, things would settle in. They had to.

In the past decade, life had twisted up and down and around like a roller coaster. Upon graduating, Greta slid into a string of long-term sub positions until she earned a place in her own classroom, at last. But then the passing of her mother crippled her, robbing her of any joy the small-town girl had managed to scrape together.

Just when it felt like she'd have to throw in the towel and move in with her father in order to cope, Greta met Kadan. After their first date, it occurred to her that *This is it!* Only to be forced into another substitute job until her current situation materialized. At times, Greta felt like life was living her rather than the other way around. Like she was a herky-jerky car hooked onto the roller coaster tracks rather than the eager amusement park guest looking for a thrill.

That attitude, of course, would get her nowhere, as her brother often reminded her. He had little patience for Greta's spells of self-pity. Truth be told, even Greta herself had little patience for her own doldrums.

Rhett had long been a source of stability. He set a high bar in school and sports, establishing a standard to which Greta's teachers and coaches would hold her accountable. At the time, it felt a little useless that Greta made all As and Bs in school. She had no plans to pursue higher education.

In fact, back when she was still in high school, Rhett was the one who pushed her to give college a chance. He had dropped out himself, and since their parents were distracted with *their* parents, who were ailing, Greta hadn't given much thought to life after senior year.

One day, she had confessed to her older brother, who by then had launched himself into the world of construction and property management, that she didn't want to work at all. She wanted to have babies and cook dinners, and that was that.

He'd chuckled at her notion, but never invalidated it (after all, Rhett himself longed for the same traditional life they'd enjoyed during their childhood—with a mom who stayed home and fussed over them and a father who made a good wage and provided modestly).

But with no romantic prospects in Hickory Grove, Greta's plan was dead in the water.

That's when Rhett cracked an idea. She could be a teacher. That way, if she met someone (apparently college was actually *less* about the learning and more about the lovin', as her freshman year roommate so eloquently put it), her schedule would be family friendly. And if she *didn't* meet anyone, she'd get to be around kids all day.

It was the perfect solution. So, she took out a boatload of student loans and enrolled at the University of Louisville, ready to study the art of meeting eligible bachelors in her classes.

Quickly, Greta realized there was far more to college life than assessing her classmates on their breeding potential. Once she began her degree coursework, she fell in love with the content. Classics, which had generally eluded her throughout high school, turned into mainstays on her nightstand, replacing her grocery aisle tabloids and EASY! crossword puzzles. The poems of Robert Frost whispered to her soul, carrying her through the hard times and lifting her spirits when the various college boys she'd met were little more than frat rats who wanted the one thing Greta was sure she did *not* want. At least, not then. Not yet.

And writing, which had only ever been a function in Greta's life, turned into a hobby. She journaled, she penned short stories, and she even sent editorials into The Vermillion. Her most popular piece was a call to bring back traditional dating. She'd titled it *Courtship for Co-eds*. It was also the piece that earned her the most hate email. Greta didn't mind. She didn't have much to lose. Not a social life, sadly. And not any prestige, either. She was just an average English Education student looking for a husband while falling in love with the Romantics. It didn't matter if her peers didn't appreciate her. Nobody had given Thoreau much never mind, either.

Her education classes added pragmatism to her creative studies. Lesson plan writing, curriculum mapping, and rubric design offered an end-goal to her journey through the world of literature and language. Suddenly, she didn't just have her own ruminations. Suddenly, Greta realized she could share her new-found love with others. She could have a captive audience.

It's why she opted for secondary rather than elementary, in the end. Greta's hope was to have moving discussions with the next generation of thinkers. She pictured herself sitting on a metal stool in the center of a ring of old-fashioned desks, ideas whipping by as she called on raised hands.

The real world, however, disappointed her. Schools didn't want Freedom Writers, they wanted data. They wanted buzz-words and call logs and tech-savvy teachers with twenty-first century skills.

It was in her first long-term substitute job that Greta learned this. The truth of education didn't, at first, discourage her. She fought it and found like-minded co-workers and inspirational administrators. She learned that it wasn't faculty members and school leaders who thought test scores reigned king. It was society. *That's* when the discouragement hit. It was also when Greta realized she might like to return to her initial goal:

finding a mate. Settling down. Baking bon-bons and charioting a carpool. Slicing up oranges for the baseball team. Then, she could read in her spare time and have it all. Maybe she'd write, too. Maybe she'd turn to substituting as a way to stay in touch.

Things got muddled somewhere. They turned backwards. Instead of searing off into a passionate career and settling comfortably into part-time classroom work, the opposite developed. Her attachment to Kadan, which began as a tepid first date, evolved into some form of commitment until they framed out a life. In Greta's eyes, it could be the perfect life. But Kadan's commitment grew tired, and their entire relationship turned delicate. Greta came to realize that it was an act. Her *own* act, at that. For whom, she wasn't sure. Did she want her mom to look down from Heaven and breathe easy? Did she want to make her dead mother happy?

Was a stale-from-the-start marriage the only way to feel personal pride? To feel like her mother was smiling down?

Hopefully not.

Presently, Greta was poised to return to her professional focus with a new passion. Sure, it might not yield a husband and babies and bon-bons. But it could satisfy her for the time being. Anyway, Greta's hopes and dreams weren't going *anywhere*. They'd be there while she found her footing back in Hickory Grove. They'd be waiting. Elsewhere, probably. But they'd be waiting. Greta wasn't despondent yet. She was a woman on a mission.

***

After wrapping up another useless effort to reach out to some connection in the world of education, Greta tossed her phone into her purse on the passenger seat and pulled into the parking lot of Mally's. The heart of Hickory Grove, Mally's was the only logical place to meet her brother and discuss plans. On their earlier call, he'd indicated he'd bring Maggie, too.

Rhett's truck sat beneath an oak tree at the far side of the parking lot, away from anyone who might pull up beside him and ding his door. *Predictable*. Greta grinned to herself and parked two spaces over, pulling forward into the dirt lot behind Mally's. She pushed out of her sedan, stood up from her car, and stretched in the warmth of the afternoon. It was nice to be a little farther south, where the sun burned hotter and the accents drawled thicker.

Kadan was an east coast transplant. His vowels and consonants came out crisp and businessy. At first, she liked how he spoke. He reminded her of some Wall Street guy with things to do and places to go. Smart and savvy. Over time, the staccato syllables and fast clip of his speech grew to be an irritant, and she found herself asking him to slow down or repeat himself as though she were an idiot.

Greta glanced back to the moving trailer she'd rented. Had she not sold off her already-second-hand furniture, she would have had to enlist Rhett to come move her. But a fresh start was a fresh start, and if she'd be holing up in Maggie Engel's barn for a month or more, then it'd be best to show up with less.

Just as Greta mounted the sidewalk toward the front of the diner, the door popped open. The clang of the bell above drew her attention to the exiting patrons, and she braced herself for a run-in with a local from her past.

The first figure was a man, tall and dressed neatly in Wranglers and a polo. Entirely unfamiliar. Behind him, a younger man, closer in age to Greta, strode out. Also tall, he wore a crisp white t-shirt and athletic shorts. Long tanned legs stretched down into smart-looking tennis shoes. He could have been a model for a sports catalog. Greta's breath caught in her throat and her hand flew to her blonde waves, scrunching them, and then to her eyes, where she rubbed the corners to clear any eyeliner smudges.

The second man noticed her, too, his gaze holding hers. She lifted her mouth in a smile just in time for Rhett to appear in the open doorway.

Her eyes flicked to her brother, and the stranger's followed.

"Greta!" Rhett's entire face lit up and he opened his arms, moving toward her just as she caught sight of the stranger, who by then had assessed the situation, turned his head, and left.

She swallowed and smiled back at Rhett. "I missed you," she replied to him as he wrapped her in his burly embrace.

They had seen each other just a couple of months earlier, but the intervening time had felt long. A lot had happened. For both of them.

"Is Maggie here?" Greta glanced back to the parking lot as she and her brother moved inside, but the man had disappeared entirely. It was just as well.

"Yes." He pointed at a booth to the far right, where Maggie sat, chatting cheerily with the waitress, who was a near spitting image of Rhett's girlfriend.

"Is that..."

Rhett replied, finishing her sentence. "Yes, that's Maggie's daughter. Gretchen. You'll love her."

Greta put on a bright smile as they neared the table for Rhett to make introductions.

Something felt off, though. In spite of their similar names and soon-to-be similar addresses, the teenager couldn't seem to shake a scowl. She reminded Greta of a mean girl, beautiful and prickly.

Still, Greta tried. "Nice to meet you, Gretchen. I've heard a lot of good things about you from my brother."

The girl's manners prevailed. She offered a weak smile. "Mr. Rhett is a good man." Then, Gretchen averted her gaze, pretending to review an order on her little notepad.

Even Maggie must have noticed it, because she all but shooed Gretchen off to the kitchen to get their drinks.

Greta took a deep breath and smiled at her brother's new girlfriend. Memories from middle school flooded her brain. Rhett and Maggie spent a lot of time together back then. They never officially dated, but Greta could recall praying that they would. Maggie would make for such a fun older sister. She slid from the booth and held her arms out to Greta, wrapping her into a warm hug.

She smelled like apple cinnamon butter.

"It's so darn good to see you, girl." Maggie bit her lower lip and studied Greta, who felt naked beneath the woman's gaze, but not as naked as Maggie's fresh face. Time ought to have dulled her vibrant red hair and washed away her freckles, but it hadn't. Wild locks zigzagged around her bright, speckled cheekbones.

"It's good to see you, too, Maggie." They sat as Greta threw a sidelong glance at Rhett, who stood by like a proud father. He had every right to be proud. He was off to the races, building his own place out in the sticks and dating the woman of his dreams all the while running his Louisville properties and helping Maggie turn her new farmhouse into a dream house. Greta was proud of him.

"Okay, should we shoot the spud or get down to business?" Maggie opened a menu then slapped it shut and tossed it back to the table. "I seem to forget that I know this menu backwards and front."

Greta laughed and cracked open her own laminated booklet, scanning for comfort food before recalling that Mally's *only* served comfort food. In fact, comfort food was about all Hickory Grove folks knew how to whip up. Carbs, butter, and a drizzle of sugar, the staples. *And* a mason jar of sweet tea.

"I'm game for whatever." Greta felt her words begin to slope out as she got her accent back. It wouldn't take long until she was singing about a holler log down by the crick. Gretchen returned with a round of tea, took their orders, then left again.

Maggie threw up her hands and sighed. "That girl has never in her life given me an attitude. Or anyone else for that matter. She'll settle in, though." She winked at Greta.

Rhett cleared his throat and lowered his voice. "Maybe this isn't a good idea, Mags."

Greta's gaze flew to Maggie, who dipped her chin and replied, "It'll be fine."

Out of the loop and now embarrassed, Greta cut in. "I'm sorry, is the barn—am I *intruding*?" Her face grew hot, and she sank back in her seat, feeling like an interloper in her older brother's business. Her older brother who meant well but possibly overstepped his boundaries. Greta stared hard at him, willing him to come clean.

Rhett held up his hands and looked at Maggie. "Hey, now. Greta can stay with me out on the new build if necessary. She won't mind a camper until something better comes along." Rhett himself had stayed in the barn for a little while as they made necessary improvements on the farm. But once things were in order, he took up in his modest R.V., which he'd parked at the lot where he was building a cabin for himself.

Lifting in her seat and leaning forward, Maggie jabbed a finger at Greta. "You are staying in our barn, and that's the *end* of it, Greta Houston." A pink grin formed on her lips and she raised her eyebrows to Rhett. "I don't want to hear another word from either of you."

Rhett and Greta exchanged a smile, too. She eased back. It was nice to have a southern mama put her in her place for once. Forced hospitality. Something Greta needed right about then.

But later, after chicken-fried steak and two glasses of sweet tea, when she and Rhett had a brief moment of privacy as Maggie used the restroom, Greta needled her brother.

"What's going on with Gretchen and the barn?" she asked in a low voice.

Rhett glanced back then leaned closer. "Gretchen was going to move into it. At least, she wanted to. She likes to sew and do projects. I think it was going to be her studio or something. But when you called, Maggie changed the whole thing on the spot. She's a bit of a bleeding heart for scorned women." He gave her a knowing look.

Heat crawled up Greta's neck and she glared back at him. "*Rhett*, this will be *so* awkward."

He shrugged and shook his head. "Maggie's the boss."

Rhett paid the bill, and they bid Gretchen a quick farewell then left. The brief memory of the strange, handsome man returned to Greta as the bell clanged above their heads, but she shook it once they started toward their vehicles.

The plan was for Greta to follow Rhett and Maggie to the farm. She could get situated immediately.

But Greta wasn't too sure that was a good idea anymore. It was one thing to accept an invitation if the space was *available*. It was quite another to dash the hopes of a teenager who liked to wield sewing needles.

Chapter 4—Luke

Over the next few days, sleep eluded Luke. Guilt and confusion washed together at night, materializing as brief, horrific nightmares.

He called out of school for the week, though really, he should have gone in and pushed through. Teaching may have been a good distraction.

Liesel had taken the reins on funeral planning, but Luke still showed up for that, drained of energy and quiet.

Truthfully, he ought to have been well prepared to arrive at the hospital and handle it. He should have known that his life would be vivisected yet again.

Just like it had when his dad died. There was the beforetime and the after.

Still, despite her blood clot and extended hospital stay, the beforetime in the case of his Mamaw felt bizarrely mundane. He was eating lunch with Mark, complaining about bus duty and lesson plans. He paid his bill. He took note of a pretty stranger and then strolled to his truck in disappointment after he witnessed her reunite with a boyfriend. He followed the speed limit all the way to Hickory Grove Regional Medical Center, playing '90s country music and tapping his thumb on the steering wheel.

It turned out that Liesel had dramatically downplayed the situation. All she asked him to do was come to the hospital. So, he did.

He arrived at the same exact time as Father Van, the parish priest from Little Flock. They rode up in the elevator together.

Even then, however, Luke did not connect the dots. When, in eerie silence, the two walked in tandem to the same hospital room, it finally clicked.

Luke fell apart. Throughout the Last Rites, Luke and Liesel sobbed without restraint.

Even during the funeral, which drew in a modest but faithful crowd of mourners (mostly relatives and even his own mother), the experience felt both uncomfortably intimate and strangely remote. Perhaps the issue was that Luke compared it to his father's funeral, in which he was the heart of everything. The well-wishers and the grief were all his.

At Mamaw Hart's funeral, the grief was more Liesel's. Liesel, his spinster aunt in her too-perfect funeral ensemble of black lace and buggy sunglasses. She was crushed, no doubt about that. But she was, well, *ready*. And Mamaw was even Liesel's own *mother*. He started wondering if death grew easier with time. It was a thought that haunted him, playing a stark reminder that Luke had hardly even lived yet.

The following week, he threw himself into work, calling the football team out of their summer break for two-a-days and staying up until ten watching tape.

By late June, he was prepared for the new school year, even if it wasn't starting for another two months. However, he was not prepared for the phone call he'd get from Zack Durbin.

Zack was a local family law attorney who, apparently, Mamaw Hart had hired to handle her final affairs.

"Zack, hi. How are you?" Initially, Luke figured Zack was calling to check in. That's how small towns worked after all. People cared. And Zack and Luke were no strangers.

Soon enough, he learned there was more to the phone call than a show of sympathy.

If Luke had the emotional energy, he'd bluff and claim that he was *managing* or some fancy word. But he was *not* managing. "It's been a bad week."

On the other end of the line, Zack cleared his throat. "I know. I'm real sorry, Luke." He cleared his throat again. "Listen, I have Liesel here with me, in my office. Your grandmother had indicated Liesel would serve as the executor for her estate, so we are going through various documents."

"Right," Luke replied, trying to shake out his tension by tossing a baseball up and catching it in a mitt. The first summer school session had just wrapped up, and the entire month of July stretched before him. He was less interested in his free time than usual and had already begun to jump ahead in his mind to other chores he might take on. Plus, he wasn't dumb. Luke figured Liesel would need his help. "Did Liesel get the bed-and-breakfast? I meant to touch base with her about it. I'm happy to help put it on the market or do whatever she'd like to get situated." It was true. He did intend to bring it up to his aunt. Just as soon as he was certain he wouldn't break into sobs talking to her. Their light text messages over the past week had been limited to the basics. Nothing regarding an estate. But Luke knew it would come up. Maybe he'd get his granddad's tools. Or even Mamaw's Buick. But those things just weren't on his mind. In fact, he was actively pushing them *out* of his mind.

He secured the ball in the mitt with a rubber band, snapping it in place then tossing it into a nearby chair as he stood and stretched.

"Actually, it might be a good idea for you to come up to my office. It doesn't have to be now, but we need to square a few things away. There is some paperwork for you, and yes—the bed-and-breakfast requires a conversation, too."

A sigh slipped between Luke's lips, and he pushed a fist into his lower back, turning into a stretch. "I'm free now."

***

Less than fifteen minutes later, Luke was sitting in an uncomfortable chair next to his aunt, whose red-rimmed eyes betrayed her composure. He'd offered her a hug before he sat but kept his gaze away. If he and Liesel had looked at each other, it'd be all over for him, too.

"Thanks for coming in, Luke." Zack steepled his fingers over a thick leather binder. "Liesel has asked me to share the breakdown, so I figure I'll get started. Is that all right?"

Luke nodded, frowning to himself.

"Your grandmother was a smart lady. She earmarked the lion share of her personal effects for the two of you." The lawyer nodded to Liesel and Luke in turn. "I have a pretty clear list of who gets what regarding her heirlooms, photo albums, furniture, and so forth. Liesel has been assigned the Buick."

Luke's head snapped up, surprised though not disappointed. "Oh?"

His aunt glanced at him, a small smile spreading across her face. "I'm happy to sell it to you for a reasonable price."

He grinned back and shook his head. "That's okay. I've got my truck."

"However, your grandmother was more ambiguous in the endowment of her income property, The Hickory Grove Inn and the home behind it."

Mamaw and Grandad Hart had inherited the bed-and-breakfast and the next-door residential property from Mamaw's parents. Mamaw lived in the second property until very recently, at which point she let it sit, hopeful that they'd find someone to live there and run the front desk.

To Luke, that plan sounded like something straight out of an Alfred Hitchcock Film. Liesel, however, liked the idea of keeping the place in the family but at arm's length.

The Hickory Grove Inn prided itself on being the best lodging in town. It kept to an outdated hospitality model in which guests could only register by phone or in person. Rooms rented cheaply on a nightly basis, and a full breakfast was served every morning. Mamaw had also offered an afternoon tea and evening sherry and dessert. Quaint didn't quite describe the whole experience, or so Luke was told by those he knew who'd stayed there.

In more recent years, there was talk of Mamaw selling the place—Liesel's idea after it quickly became clear that there was a shortage in the workforce. No one in town who led so simple a life that they could give it all up for a local landmark that didn't even belong to them.

Mamaw didn't agree and felt the place ought to go directly to her descendants. Unfortunately, there were only two of those left, and neither one was the type to take on a bed-and-breakfast. Liesel, despite her perfect exterior and vicious drive, focused on the church. All of her energy went into Little Flock.

Every last ounce. Despite being unwed and childless, her heart and time were spoken for.

Luke, on the other hand, had the time. Plus, his heart wasn't yet spoken for. But, well, he was a thirty-something-year-old guy who preferred tinkering over simple chores like changing the oil in his truck and mowing the grass in his free time. Not passing out brochures and positioning squares of chocolate on some stranger's pillow. He was more HGTV than Hallmark. Leaky pipe? He'd handle it. Decorate the gift shop for Christmas? Hard pass.

He swallowed and exchanged another look with Liesel. Her eyebrows had furrowed, and lines formed like rivulets on her forehead. Liesel had always held age at bay, keeping clear of the sun (though her naturally olive complexion would suggest otherwise) and watching what she ate. She kept fashionable despite a modest income as the secretary and religious education director for Little Flock Catholic.

"What do you mean *ambiguous*?" Luke asked.

"She didn't specify an heir."

"It goes to Liesel, though. Right?" He hooked a thumb at his aunt, whose expression turned unreadable. She licked her lips and shrugged her shoulders. "Shouldn't it be Liesel? Ma-maw's *daughter*?"

"Well, it's the reason the estate has fallen into probate. We have to come to an agreement on what happens to the place."

The answer was simple. Bed and breakfasts weren't for men. He wasn't the type who could turn a bed or work a cash register. He didn't know diddly squat about the hospitality business.

Then again, maybe Liesel didn't, either.

"You can list the properties and split the profit once they sell. Your mamaw owned it free and clear." Zack leaned back, one hand outspread as if it was the only option. As if this was all simple and quick.

Twisting in his seat, Luke pinned his aunt with a hard stare. "Is that the right choice? What if we try again to find someone to help run the place? Maybe Stella could take on the night-shift in the interim. Or, if she can't do it, I suppose I could stay there the rest of the summer. Until school starts." They had hired Stella, a kindly local, to run the front desk. She began once Mamaw moved from the house next to the Inn into the assisted living facility. She was no work horse, but she got them through. But she alone wouldn't be enough. Liesel had filled in where she could, but the place really needed a live-in property manager.

Liesel shook her head. "That's a short-term solution, Luke."

"Maybe we *should* sell." Luke felt a knot form in his throat. If they were discussing this pre-Mamaw's death, he'd feel more secure in that decision. But now, with his only direct ancestral link to the Hart family dead and gone, he felt differently. Anxious about the right path. Uncertain about the future. Everything flipped now that it was *after*.

Liesel squeezed her eyes shut and delicately pressed the pad of her ring finger to the corner of each.

"What about Grandad's brothers and sisters? Is there someone who might have a serious interest?" Luke asked.

"Gary Hart." Liesel heaved a deep sigh after the name fell from her mouth.

Even Zack grimaced.

Luke just shook his head then looked up at Zack. "Has Gary asked about it?"

When Zack glanced to his right then down at the leather binder, Luke had his answer.

"It can't go to Gary, Liesel," Luke pleaded.

She nodded quietly. "I agree. But it's a big commitment, Luke. I would do it if I could, but... oh, I don't know. I hate to see someone else take the place. I mean, I know I wanted that a while back, but..." her voice trailed off and tears began a slow descent down her cheeks. She didn't bother to brush them away and instead folded her arms over her chest, sobbing quietly.

Luke reached out, offering his hand to his aunt. She took it, and he squeezed gently. "Zack," he began, forcing himself to keep it together. "I'll take care of The Hickory Grove Inn. We'll keep it. We have to."

But the lawyer didn't seem satisfied. "This could be complicated. The deed can, technically, go into both of your names. Are you sure you want that? It would tie you both to the properties, for better or worse."

Liesel lifted her shoulders weakly. "If we don't keep it, Gary Hart will buy it. You know he will. He'll turn it into a gym or an office space, and *poof*. There goes the past."

And just like that, Luke's summer was spoken for.

Chapter 5—Greta

About two weeks had passed since Greta had taken residence in the Engel-Devereux family barn. There, she helped tend to the land and the animals. Goats and chickens. Two dogs and a cat with her kittens. If it weren't for the ever-growing tension with Gretchen, Greta might have liked to stay on longer. Even as a girl, she'd always liked housework. It brought her a sense of calm. Every Friday, as a young woman, she'd do light cleaning for her grandparents. They paid her ten dollars a week, but Greta would have done it for free. There, she would make the beds, tidy the kitchen, and add little touches here and there—if Greta hadn't fallen into teaching, she might have become a maid. Maybe in some southern manor somewhere. Service had long been a part of the fiber of her being, and housework particularly filled that calling.

Working outside at Maggie's quickly took on the shape of therapy for her, allowing for the chance to process her life, reflect on where things soured with Kadan (spoiler: they'd started off as being sour).

And while she raked the back field, she practiced her answers to interview questions.

Interviews that hadn't yet been scheduled.

Despite the bond that grew between Greta and Maggie and between Greta and the land, she took back up with completing online applications; first, in every district she was familiar with. But with no open secondary English positions, she had two choices: lower her standards and consider returning to long-term subbing *or* broaden her geographic scope.

After her most recent experience in the world of educational babysitting, Greta knew her only option was to look elsewhere. Dead set on returning to a big city, where she'd still have a shot at a dating life, Greta now sat behind her laptop on the futon in Maggie Devereux's barn and tapped away her responses to the online interest form for Chicago Public Schools.

Ten years' experience. Indiana State Teaching License: Secondary English Education. (She made a mental note to see about certification reciprocity between Indiana and Illinois.) Specialization in literature and language with added emphasis on reading instruction. Yes, she'd be interested in coaching an after-school sport, though her experience was limited to softball and volleyball. No, she was not familiar with ASTUTE, a state-wide assessment technology system that also offered curriculum maps, professional development webinars, data tracking, and student-friendly software. However, yes, she was a fast learner, flexible and driven.

Greta rubbed her eyes with her knuckles and hit submit on the darn thing.

CPS was an expansive district, and right then, that's the only hope she clung to. A big school system. Lots of openings. Lots of students. Lots of children who needed a teacher to inspire them and love them. Even if the inspiration would be muted by a wide-reaching technology platform.

Anxious, she closed her laptop, leaning back and stretching her legs out.

Rhett was due for supper that night, and Greta needed to shower and change. She'd spent the day cleaning the chicken coop, and she had promised Maggie she'd help prepare dinner. At every one of Greta's offers to take on this chore or head up that project, the kind mother of four insisted up and down that Greta ought to relax and enjoy herself. Go for a walk. Get a bite to eat at Mally's. But Greta refused, feeling that, for a while, she'd quite like to retreat. So long as Greta didn't have anywhere else to be, she preferred to play Transcendentalist. Maggie's farm was her Walden Pond.

***

Maggie's kids flopped in from the backyard, their shoes caked in dried mud, though it hadn't rained in recent days. Ky, the oldest of the three who lived at home, was leading the parade, a baby cat nestled in the crook of his arm. "What's for supper?"

Maggie left Greta at the stove and redirected the children back outside to hose off. "And then go through the front door so you can leave your sneakers on the porch!" Maggie's voice grew louder at the end of the sentence as the kids dashed away. "And don't forget to wash up!" she added loudly after them with a laugh.

Greta admired her. The single mom never seemed to grow impatient with her rascally brood, instead laughing off their mess-making as "*kids*!" Greta might have done well to see Maggie in action before she took on the elementary subbing gig.

"How're the taters lookin'?" she asked Greta as she transferred a steaming pot of collard greens to the center of the table.

Greta left the chicken on the stove and grabbed the bowl she'd finished whipping. "Mashed and buttery," she answered with a proud smile.

Maggie took over on the fried chicken and Greta took up with scooping creamy ladlesful onto each plate. The doorbell chimed, and a ruckus ensued. Voices mixed out on the porch.

"You all get your rear ends to the bathroom and wash up *on the double*!" Maggie hollered.

"I already washed up."

Greta's head whipped to the doorway. Her brother stood there, his hands held up in defense of himself. His eyes were on Maggie, and in his gaze, Greta thought she spied the look of a groom as his bride entered the aisle. Desire. More than that, actually. True love.

She glanced away, grinning to herself. Rhett deserved all the happiness in the world. It seemed like Maggie did, too.

***

Dinner was a boisterous affair. It began with a sweet, lumpy, rushed rendition of *grace* by Briar.

Bless us o Lord and these is my gifts from Ky bounty Christ the Lord Amen. Rushed signs of the cross morphed into a squabble about who would get the last dinner roll, which made no sense to Greta, who had baked no fewer than forty of them.

"It's *thy* bounty," Dakota corrected his little sister as he rolled a piece of his bread into a doughy lump and tossed it into his mouth. "Not *Ky* bounty." The brothers shared a laugh, but the spunky girl shrugged it off and resumed babbling to her Barbie doll.

Once tummies started to fill, and the adults wrapped up their small talk, attention turned to more serious matters. The kids kept chatting, and their previous bickering churned like butter into easy conversation about those little conspiracies children formed between each other. What traps the boys had set. Which kitten Briar had just finished bottle feeding before they dragged themselves back to the farmhouse.

Maggie smiled warmly at them then pointed a manicured finger to the empty seat, a veritable elephant in the room. "Gretchen's been taking her evening meals with Theo." She wiggled her eyebrows at Greta then Rhett.

"He's a nice kid," Rhett commented, oblivious.

"Yeah, if only his girlfriend was a nice kid, too." Maggie flicked a knowing look to Greta, who was the only one to catch the joke. But it didn't sit well with her. Why bring up the most awkward thing about their arrangement?

Dabbing her lips with her napkin, Greta spoke next. "I filled out an interest form for Chicago Public Schools today. I'm going to send my resume to some principals up there, too."

"I wish you wouldn't," Maggie replied, clicking her tongue.

Greta looked at her, trying to read between the lines. She had yet to pressure Greta to stay. So far, things felt like a pleasant arrangement, only *made* pleasant by the promise of its impermanence. "Maggie, Gretchen is sick of me being here. I have to get a plan in place sooner rather than later or else we're in danger of having a full-blown falling out."

Maggie set her fork down on her plate, and it clattered to the center, leftover butter sliding up the length of the silverware. The woman wiped her hands on her napkin and shook her head. "I wasn't trying to start trouble. I was just pointing out that maybe this was a good thing." She waved her long fingers back and forth between Greta and herself.

The three younger children fell silent, turning into an audience rather than the sideshow act.

Greta cocked her head. "What do you mean?"

"That girl was on track for working her life away. She wakes up, does some classwork for school, goes to Mally's and takes orders, gives them ten hours, heads to night school, comes home and does more coursework then starts all over again. Once she got together with Theo, he was little more than a footnote in her phone. And if Gretchen *had* moved into that barn, if just to set up her little sewing studio, it'd go to waste. She'd still be working all day, rolling in late with her nose in a book, and falling asleep well before she ever sat down at a sewing machine. One, which, by the way, we can't even find all the parts for." They'd been down this road. Maggie complained about her daughter's work ethic every second of every day. "I just want her to have a little fun, but I can't seem to convince her to slow down."

"It's because you're her mom," Greta replied evenly. "She needs to hear it from someone else."

Maggie lifted an eyebrow to her other children, who were rapt with this lesson in family dynamics. "So, is that also why Dakota and Ky can't be convinced to do their homework? Because it's their mama who tells them to?"

The table erupted in laughter, and all was well again.

School was one arena in which Greta was supremely comfortable. She took a long swig of her sweet tea then braved the waters of opening a conversation with an adolescent boy. "Ky, what books did you read in English class last year?"

He took an oversized bite of chicken, the crispy crumbles sticking to the corners of his mouth as he shrugged his shoulders. "I don't remember. Some story about a boy named Jonas." He swallowed but didn't bother to wipe his face. "Oh, yeah. We had to read *The Secret Garden* which the girls liked, but it was a kids' book to me."

"That does sound a little young for a middle schooler," Maggie added thoughtfully.

Greta shrugged, trying to take up for the poor teacher who surely had a good reason. "It's a classic. You're never too old to read a classic."

"That's true. And the school and teachers are terrific, truly. It's just that since I don't know how to help them learn the difference between commas and a scratch on the paper, they might fall behind. Will they be prepared?" Maggie asked pointedly.

Greta restrained herself from rolling her eyes. "Depends on how the teacher had them study it. I'd say it's more about the *how* rather than the *what* when it comes to instruction and curriculum."

"Maybe you could tutor Ky and Dakota this summer," Rhett offered. He meant well, Greta was sure, but even Maggie cringed.

"I'd love that. But, Rhett, look at your sister. Greta does enough around here. She doesn't need to wrangle these heathens in their academics. Ky will have another English class again next year, with Ms. Randall. And I'm sure she will fill in any gaps or whatever you education people call it."

Greta tried to redirect the conversation, rising from her seat so she could bring dessert over.

But Ky grunted. "Ms. Randall isn't gon' be there next year."

"What?" Maggie asked, frowning. "What do you mean?"

Greta's ears pricked up.

"She's getting married to somebody in Louisville and moving." He went back to eating but a flash lit up his face. "Hey! Wait a minute! Maybe they'll just cancel Language Arts! Maybe I won't have to take it at all!"

Maggie smacked her hand down on the table in front of her oldest son. "Ky," she glanced back at Greta, who'd returned with an apple pie. "Are you positive?"

Ky looked from Maggie to Greta to Rhett, his face a chubby ball of furrows and confusion. "Maybe. Maybe they'll just tell my class to read a book for Language Arts."

Rhett chuckled, and Greta smiled, but Maggie shook her head before it flopped backwards in aggravation. "That's not what I'm talking about, young man. I'm asking you if Ms. Randall really did quit her job."

The lightbulb flickered in his little boy brain, and a slow smile crept across his lips. "You're talkin' about if there's gonna be a teaching job there? At Hickory Grove Middle?"

Greta just shook her head. "Surely, they have more than one English—er, *Language Arts*—class per grade level?"

Though, even when she attended H.G.M.S., there was only one teacher per grade. Small rural school, that's what you got.

Maggie wordlessly raised an eyebrow to Greta then pinned her gaze back on her son. "Yes, little boy blue, that's what Mama's saying." She wagged her hand in lazy circles to drag more information out. But boys Ky's age were notoriously useless at gossip.

He hooked a fleshy finger at Greta. How that child could be pudgy was both bewildering and perfectly sensible. Though he played hard all the day long, he ate hard at every meal, with snacks in between. Rhett had said that ever since Maggie had taken up in the farmhouse, it was part hair salon, part Cracker Barrel. *She ought to name it Maggie's Cut and Crunch.* It was a lame joke, but Greta began to see how true it rang. All throughout helping Maggie fix supper, every single day she was there, they had to repurpose the whole kitchen space, air it out with long dish towels and open windows, light half a dozen candles, preheat the oven with that morning's bacon pan then move the supplies to the parlor, which Maggie eventually intended to turn into her shop. Just as soon as Rhett could get a plumbing fixture in there.

"Are you asking if I could get Miss Greta a job at my school?" Ky asked.

Rhett belted out a laugh and reached across the table to scruff the kid's hair.

Maggie just shook her head and held her hands to God to save her from her misery. "Oh, Lordy. Ky, you just kill me." At length, she and Greta also laughed, but Greta's died off faster.

"Ky, I'd love to be your teacher." She sliced into the pie, dividing it into six equal triangles before sliding each one onto the waiting dessert plates. "But I can't."

"Oh, come on Greta. What are you talking about? If Ky here knows what he's talking about, then there is an English position right under your nose, for goodness' sake!"

Greta blinked and fell into her chair, stabbing at her pie and shaking her head. "*Language Arts*," she corrected him under her breath.

"Huh?" Rhett asked.

Greta held up a hand toward Ky. "It's *Language Arts*, not English. I'm a high school English teacher."

"Sweetheart," Maggie rested her hand on Greta's forearm, squeezing it warmly. "I mean this to be as kind as I possibly can. You're not a high school English teacher, Greta Houston. You're a broken heart. You're a little sister. You're a houseguest and a farmhand. You're a neat-freak and a hard worker. You're a small-town girl who found her way home and yet you've got your sights set on some big city school up north. Why? So that you can say you're a high school English teacher? Honey, you don't know *what* in the heck you are."

Chapter 6—Luke

The Hickory Grove Inn had turned into nothing short of a hot mess. Liesel didn't shed any of her church responsibilities, and so Luke was alone in learning about how to run the darn place. Stella showed him all she knew, but that turned out to be relatively little.

With his aunt, it was always *I'll come by later* or *I trust your judgement, just make the call*. He'd had to give one set of weekend guests his phone number instead of Liesel's for any overnight emergencies, which gave him hives. To be on call for strangers felt intrusive.

Finally, after a couple weeks of driving back and forth from his house to the bed-and-breakfast, he ended up camping out in his grandmother's little house next door. That proved even harder, and he learned very quickly why Liesel was so hands-off.

Mamaw Hart was *everywhere* there. From her afghans to her Tupperware, he couldn't escape the woman's ghost. The sadness he thought he might have overcome by putting in extra time on some repairs at the Inn returned with a sharp vengeance, needling him to the point where he finally called a *business meeting* with his aunt.

"This is too hard," he began, as they stood outside his house up on Lowell Avenue. She had an accounting appointment for Little Flock, and he had been called to sit in on a couple of interviews. He and Liesel had exactly ten minutes, and he should have just taken her to dinner to sort things out, but, well, Luke was fed up. "School starts in a couple of weeks, and by then I can't be on call. You're busy too, Aunt Liesel, I get that. Still, something's got to change."

"We said we'd hire someone," Liesel replied, checking her wristwatch compulsively.

"Mamaw's stuff's still in that house. We can't hire someone for *that*. We need to set aside time to go in there *together* and sort through it. We need to *commit*."

He felt foolish being the one to come down hard on his elder, but it had to be said. If his own aunt couldn't step up to the plate, then Luke was lost. Frustrated. At his wits' end.

"Fine." She threw up her hands but then drew one down to rub under her eye. Her voice rattled. "We'll clean it out. We'll hire a live-in manager. Just say when and what, and I'll do it."

He blew air through tight lips. "Let's meet there tomorrow evening. I'll see if I can bring Mark to help with moving stuff. We can store as much as possible in my shed. In the meantime, can you add the job posting to the parish bulletin?"

She nodded her head in one quick bob and agreed to the plan.

Satisfied that there was a light at the end of the tunnel, Luke took off, dialing Mark as he walked the short distance to school.

"Hey, Mark. Any chance you're free tomorrow night? Aunt Liesel and I are going to start sorting through Mamaw's stuff, and we might need help with heavy lifting. She's... she's not taking it very well."

"I'll be there. Say, I'm just finishing some new plays. Can you meet me at Mally's to go over them?"

"I'm heading in to help with the interviews. Afterwards?"

Mark agreed, and Luke ended the call, rolling his shoulders back into place and redirecting his attention on the task at hand: ensuring Hickory Grove Middle School did not hire another faculty member who was charmed by the small town life but unwilling to stick it out.

***

The first interviewee was a middle-aged woman from Corydon. It did not go well. Several times throughout the fifteen-minute Q&A session, Luke felt himself forcibly holding back a need to bite down on his fist. She had all the prerequisites, her certification and fingerprint clearance card. But her reason for applying, which she made crystal clear, was her dissatisfaction with her current position. She'd accidentally shown *The Scarlet Letter* film (the one from the nineties that was rated R) in its entirety to a classroom full of ninth graders. She'd been reprimanded and was happy to share all the gory details during the length of her time with the Hickory Grove hiring committee.

When they thanked her for coming in, Mrs. Cook, a former English teacher herself, murmured that *The Scarlet Letter* wasn't usually taught in ninth grade to begin with.

Luke, who had read only a handful of books in his whole life, felt a little out of the loop on that angle, but he still took his job of helping to round out the committee by offering a male's perspective. "She was confident," he added as professionally as he could, "but this community is somewhat conservative. I doubt they would like for their children to be a captive audience to on-screen nudity."

The others nodded in agreement. A few snickered. Luke would, too, if Mark was there to josh with. But generally, he preferred to keep things above board. His title as a phys. ed. teacher already set him apart as less serious about the job, and he didn't want to contribute to that if he could help it. Plus, he believed what he said. If he had a young daughter, he'd want a competent teacher. Not someone who didn't properly vet her media before a lesson. Sure, mistakes happened. But that woman was a train wreck. Thank goodness there was a second applicant.

Mrs. Cook left to bring her in, the second (and *final*) candidate. If this one was even one degree better than the last, they'd probably offer her a job on the spot.

"Houston," Mrs. Crabapple announced, reading from the printed resume they'd each received a copy of. "That name doesn't sound familiar. Do you know the *Houston* family, Coach?" She coughed into her fist. Mrs. Crabapple was the only other staff member present who had grown up in the county, but she wasn't a true local. She was from River Port, a tiny community on the banks of the Ohio. "Ladies? Any of you all?" She looked around the small group of teachers, but her gaze landed back on Luke and she shifted in her seat, tucking her hands beneath her bosom and lacing them together on her ample stomach.

Luke shrugged. "It's a common name. Feel like I might have run into someone by the name but not too sure."

He hadn't yet studied the paperwork and, for some reason, expected to look down and see the name of a man. However, Luke didn't have a chance to confirm his suspicion, because she appeared right then, in the doorway ahead of Mrs. Cook. *She.* Not *he.*

The fact that she was a woman was not, however, the detail that shocked him the most.

It was that this Houston woman, this—he glanced down at the thick white page in his hand, blinking before returning his eyes to her face—this *Ms. Greta Houston* was strikingly familiar.

Chapter 7—Greta

It was all wrong. Middle school language arts? And in *Hickory Grove*? The *only* reason Greta agreed to apply for the position and accept an interview was to keep Maggie and Rhett happily out of her business.

What it came to feel like was that they were squarely inside of her business. Directing it, even. With Maggie, she didn't mind so much. But with Rhett, Greta had the compulsion to turn back into her pre-teen self and tell him to *bug out!* or *get lost!*

Still, to see the hope in Ky, Dakota, *and* Briar's little faces that Miss Greta might one day be their teacher... it was too much to ignore. However, there was Gretchen to think of. Gretchen hadn't yet heard the news that Greta was thinking of staying in Hickory Grove. Would it upset her further? Would she assume that Greta would stay in the barn for the long haul?

She wouldn't, of course. Because, for goodness' sake, Greta was *not* taking a middle school *language arts* job in a town that barely had a stoplight, much less a dating scene.

She would do it to keep them quiet and placid as she rooted around harder for something else. Anyway, it didn't hurt to start practicing her interview skills. But that night, Greta swore to herself she'd stop being so lackadaisical and really get down to business, scouring the internet for school districts and opening her mind to different cities. Different districts. She'd even follow up with Chicago Public Schools by personally reaching out to principals. That way she wasn't lost in a backlog of online interest forms.

In the meantime, Greta would go into her old middle school, pray she didn't know anyone on the hiring committee, make a half-hearted attempt to answer their questions, then get out of there. After all, she was still within the window for Chicago Public to get back to her *without* her reaching out to the principals. The online confirmation message promised a turn-around time of responding to her inquiry within one week. It was about to be one week.

Also, summer was nearly over. But that was a thought Greta simply pushed aside. Worst case scenario, she'd find a normal district. One where you started school in September, not *August*, for goodness' sake!

Still, despite all of the reasons she should not teach in Hickory Grove, and despite her very vocal insistence that she was doing it *just because I love you guys* and *it'll be good interview practice anyway*, a quieter, smaller voice from deep inside of her pushed on her heart, reminding her of the truth that she learned long, long before. *When God closes a door, he opens a window*. It was up to Greta to listen to that quiet, small voice. After all, even if she had better opportunities elsewhere, a bird in the hand was worth two in the bush.

Right?

It was the quiet, small voice that guided her through getting ready and putting together an outfit: a summery-but-serious pink chiffon dress with cap sleeves and a hemline that hit in the dead center of her knees and sensible-if-stylish espadrille wedges. She applied light makeup and drew wisps of her chunky blonde waves back from their typical position along her temples, pinning them in place with a pale pink barrette.

Greta wouldn't normally select pink for an interview. Green or red, or even black, sure. But she couldn't find her dressy blouses, and it was too hot for slacks. Anyway, she was often told that pink was *her color*, and her mother had always said that if you're lucky enough to *have a color*, you simply must own it. So, with little to lose anyway, Greta did just that.

Maggie let her get ready in her bathroom rather than in front of the small mirror in the barn, but both locales were stuffy. The farmhouse was cooled by one, lone window AC unit, and so Greta had to get ready quickly enough that she could slip into her car where she'd blast the air and pray that she could stave off any anxiety sweat for the duration of the drive and her interview.

***

Once she had parked in the front lot at Hickory Grove M.S., Greta tucked her leather attaché neatly beneath her arm. Inside of it was a tube of lipstick, her wallet, keys, and extra copies of her résumé, printed weeks earlier at Indy Print and Paper. Though she'd already emailed the same document with her application, and though, again, this whole thing was really just a practice run, it wouldn't hurt to show up prepared and snazzy. You never knew who was connected in the world of education, and she sure didn't want H.G.M.S. to spread the word that a sloppy applicant was making the rounds. Greta insisted to herself that she maintain the high level of professionalism she'd developed over the years. She might be from Hickory Grove, but even if she knew anyone on the interview team, she hoped to impress them with her worldliness.

"Hi!" Greta beamed at the secretary, who sat in front of an oscillating fan at a dated computer.

The woman tore her attention from the screen and looked up, smiling broadly. "Well, now!" she gushed as she rose and crossed to the counter behind which Greta stood. "You must be Miss Greta Houston!" Her bubbly demeanor was disarming and welcome.

"That's right," Greta replied. "I'm here for an interview with Mrs. Cook." She smoothed the fabric of her dress along her torso, feeling surprisingly at ease. It helped that the secretary was a new face. No one to embarrass herself in front of. No one to shrink in front of when they droned on about how they hadn't seen little Greta Houston since she was knee-high to a grasshopper! She let out a breath and glanced beyond the kindly woman.

"They are just finishing up with the first one. Miss Danielle—I mean, *Mrs. Cook*—will be out shortly, dear. Take a seat if you'd like." She gestured to a chair across from the counter, wooden and rigid, as old as the school building itself, no doubt. It was a wonder to Greta that the whole place didn't feel more familiar. The shape was. And if she was pressed to, she could find just about any place or anything there, from muscle memory, but the bulletin boards and the general *feel* were somehow more comfortable and welcoming now than when she was in seventh or eighth grade. Perhaps, that made perfect sense.

Greta sat and regretted it. As soon as her weight hit the seat, nerves set in. Was it the reality of an interview? Or the fact that she wasn't the lone candidate for the job? Who'd have thought Hickory Grove Middle School would have a long line of applicants? Was this Danielle Cook turning around the rural school system and drawing in fresh-faced, capable teachers from the four corners of Indiana? From across the river?

Greta closed her eyes briefly, and when she opened them, the secretary was bidding farewell to a perm-headed, slacks-wearing middle-aged woman. With a handbag slung over the shoulder of her blouse, she oozed confidence and a blasé attitude. She waved boldly at Greta. "May the odds be ever in your favor." And then, with a wink and a chuckle, she left the building.

The woman's parting line was from a YA dystopian novel that Greta had never read. Nor had she seen the movie based on said novel. She couldn't even think of the title, blanking entirely. The woman who left was clearly in the loop on all things middle school language arts. Then there was Greta, certain she was too good for the job. Too academic and competent to be reduced to simple grammar and weekly spelling tests. And yet, she couldn't even draw to her memory a blockbuster film that probably every single child in that school building was familiar with.

Did she learn *nothing* from her elementary subbing gig? Every grade level had its own demands, and there she was, pretending that her secondary English credentials would over-qualify her. She didn't stop to consider whether she might actually be *under*qualified. She swallowed past the lump in her throat just as a curvy blonde woman strode out from the hall beyond the secretary's front desk.

"You must be Greta?" The woman was classically beautiful and dressed to the nines in a pantsuit and hoop earrings. Her voice twangy but her face unfamiliar, she was southern, not lo-

cal. At least, not that Greta could pin down. The entire predic-
tion of Greta's experience so far did not ring true. What happened to the lazy rural junior high from her youth? What happened to her idea that this place would be begging for her, not
her for it?

"Yes." Greta rose and stretched out her hand too early,
walking like a goofy zombie to meet up with the woman in the
passageway to the left of the reception counter. "Mrs. Cook?"
Greta managed to squeak out as they finally connected for a
firm shake.

The woman nodded and folded her hands in front of herself. "It's wonderful to meet you. Thank you for coming in on
such short notice. I saw in your C.V. that you're from Hickory
Grove?"

Greta followed her down a stuffy hallway back to the area
where Greta, as a child, had always suspected the principal's
office sat. Her previous moment of familiarity and comfort
washed away immediately on the short walk to the back offices.
Greta felt more out of place than she ever had as an embarrassed pre-teen with a full mouth of braces and pimple-speck-
led forehead.

"That's right. Born and raised. I'm..." as she began to comb
her brain for an explanation of why she was suddenly back and
looking for a job, a white lie formed on her tongue. She hated to fib, but there was no way the interview would go well if
Greta confessed that this was all a well-intentioned ruse. "I'm
moving back home. To be near family." She swallowed then
added for the sake of her own conscience, "Depending on...
some things." Shaking her head, Greta wanted to crawl inside
her little brown satchel and disappear amongst the stubs of

Ticonderoga pencils that had surely wedged their way into the bottom folds.

"Well," Mrs. Cook turned to face Greta, her hand on a doorknob. "We are so excited to learn more about you today. Please," she opened the door and gestured inside, "come in."

Her eyes adjusted to the small room. Sunlight spilled in from a long window beyond four other faces, each partially re-clined in broad-backed rolling desk chairs. Greta's eyes passed from three women to one, lone man.

And that's when the sweat started in. Greta's throat tight-ened. Her chest tightened. Her grip on her satchel tightened to the point she thought the skin of her knuckles would crack and burst. At least it would distract from her flushed face.

It was him. The man from the diner. The impossible, dash-ing man who had locked eyes with her.

Though the other women stayed seated, he stood up, ini-tially shoving his hands into khaki pockets then passing one hand over the lower half of his face.

The others didn't seem to take notice of the quiet under-current throbbing between Greta and their colleague.

"Greta," Mrs. Cook began, gesturing to the still-seated women. "That's Mrs. Crabapple, our music teacher; Ms. Ran-dall, our exiting English teacher; Ms. O'Neal, one of our math teachers; and" — Greta could have sworn Mrs. Cook paused for effect — "This is Coach Hart, our P.E. teacher."

"Hart," Greta murmured. Her face flushed even deeper, to the point where Greta wanted to sink into the hardwood floors, seep between the cracks like dust. Her mortification caused her to nearly miss the chance to take his hand in a warm, heartachingly warm, shake. "I mean *Hart*," she tried to recover.

"Hart, like..." her brain floundered around until she thought of someone—*anyone* she knew named Hart. There were dozens of them in town. It was more prominent a family than any, probably. "Like, um. You're a Hart?" Greta's eyes fluttered closed and her fingers drifted to her forehead, covering half her face as it melted into humiliation.

Fortunately, he was able to fill in the gaps. "That's right. I didn't grow up here, though. My dad was Kurt Hart. My mom's name is May. She's out in Louisville, though."

The way he said it, that one word that only Kentuckianan's could say just right, with the syllables flopping from three to two and sliding off his tongue, co-mingling into a soft landing in the air between them... it turned her knees weak, and she plopped into the chair Mrs. Cook had gestured to.

Turning her focus to the other women and then Mrs. Cook, Greta tried her best to shake it off. Heat slid down her neck and settled on her collar bones, turning from a sheet of red into splotches. Thank goodness her neckline rose high above her chest. She could at least pretend, now, to be the professional she felt like just ten minutes before. Nodding to Coach Hart now, she replied that she went to school with some Harts.

He didn't take his eyes off of Greta, and she could feel it, but she refused to meet his gaze as he answered, "My cousins, probably."

"That's wonderful," Mrs. Cook cut in. "It's so great to have a real local. Several have retired recently, and we hope to bring a little of that flavor back to H.G.M.S. Isn't that right?" She smiled warmly around the table. If the words came out of the mouth of any other principal, they'd fall flat, like insincere schmoozing. But Mrs. Cook was as genuine as they came. Dedicated, to be sure. Happy, too. Greta saw little bits of herself in the woman. Someone who felt passionately about education.

"Let's begin with more about you, Greta," Mrs. Cook continued, settling into her own seat between Coach Hart and the math teacher.

Taking a deep breath, Greta forced her attention on the principal and answered, surprising even herself with candid descriptions of her journey back to Hickory Grove.

After Greta finished her personal overview and fielded ten generic questions, she found she was back in place. More at ease. Comfortable.

Mrs. Cook smiled again at the group then at Greta, lacing her fingers on top of the white pages in front of her. "All right, Greta, one more question from us." Greta swallowed, finally flicking a quick glance to Coach Hart. His eyes were on her, still. Had they ever left? She thought not.

She braced herself, and just as could be expected, Mrs. Cook asked the question Greta had danced around earlier. "So why Hickory Grove? Why your old stomping grounds?" The woman made a fist and swung it across her chest in an old-fashioned gesture of solidarity.

Greta took a deep breath. She had to be honest, above all else. No more half-truths or white lies. No, it wouldn't do to admit that her top choices weren't hiring (or, at least, they weren't hiring *her*).

Swallowing and glancing around the table, Greta raised her palms. "You know? H.G.M.S. was not initially on my radar. I would love to teach high school English, and the allure of the bigger cities is hard to resist for someone my age. Someone—" she threw a quick look to Coach Hart (*what was his first name! She was desperate to know!*) "Someone who hasn't settled down yet," she went on, blinking past him and finding the right words. She had their attention. You could probably hear a straw of hay land; the round oak table was so quiet. "But my brother lives here, and so do some close friends. Some, er, some people I've grown close to. Maggie Devereux and her family." She looked up, catching flickers of recognition among their faces, but still they kept quiet and waited.

"Well..." Greta paused to let out a long breath. "Well, the other night over supper, Maggie's son, Ky, told us about Ms. Randall, and they asked if I might apply. Well, you see, I wasn't too certain at first, since I really love teaching novels and po-etry. I wasn't sure if middle school would be the right fit, you know?"

Doubt swelled in her chest. Was she wrong to be so forth-coming? Was she going to shoot herself in the foot? Oh, what did it matter? She *was not* sure it was a good fit. The *only* reason she was feeling nervous now was because of the dashing stranger. He wasn't so much a stranger. He was a quiet middle school P.E. teacher. Her eyes flashed to his hands, which, like Mrs. Cook, laid patiently on the pages in front of him. Big tanned hands folded on each other. His left was resting on top of the right. On his fingers, Greta detected no rings. No *ring*.

"Anyway," she went on, clearing her throat, "The kids were so excited about it. It was *feverish*, their excitement. I realized maybe there was more to the age group than I had considered. Coming from subbing with elementary, I thought I might be scarred a little. You know, young boys and their talk of bodily functions." The table roared to life with laughter, and Greta snapped out of her winding, poorly thought out explanation. She should feel embarrassed at her admission about the boogers and bathroom jokes, but some *energy* inside had taken over. A deep-seated truth that forced its way out. Smiling back at them, she regained her footing. "But my passions are two-fold. I love English, yes, and I love the teaching of it as much or more than I *believe* in teaching. So, really, as long as I have students and books, well... I'm a happy camper."

Mrs. Cook glanced at the others, and it occurred to Greta she did not quite answer the question.

"Oh," Greta interjected, holding a finger up. "May I add one more thing?"

"Please do," Mrs. Cook replied, waving her hand generously.

"I think I answered a question that you didn't ask. If it's not obvious, I'm sort of grappling with my future a little."

The others kept mum.

"I grew up in this town with my brother. Our parents raised us here. They loved it here. We weren't a big family, but we were a happy one. Rhett—my brother that is—and I both moved away. I think we believed that happiness existed elsewhere. We wanted to see the world, I suppose. Neither of us got very far, but there you have it. Well, Rhett moved back recently. He reconnected with his old friends, the ones still in town. You know how small-town folks just seem to float away on a hope and a dream. Well, Rhett floated back. And he's just... he's just so happy. I don't know if I can find that here. But, I guess what I'm trying to say is that I know that while I might have more chances to fan out and experience the world in a big city, I know that my first goal is to be a teacher. Have a classroom.

Settle in for once. If you're willing to take a chance on me with all my hemming and hawing, well, I'd love to make a go of it here."

A smile brightened Greta's face as the words rang true. Throughout the course of the interview, it all just snapped into place for her. Like through the questions, she found a piece of herself. She couldn't make any promises, but that was all she needed: *promise*. There it was, sitting before her. The kind, committed principal, the handsome guy who, even if he alone wasn't available surely indicated that handsome guys *did* exist in Hickory Grove. And the *promise* of working with kids. Reading books like *The Secret Garden* and whatever that other end-of-the-world teen favorite was (she told herself to head directly to the library and get her hands on it).

By the time Greta wrapped up her answer, she was no longer embarrassed to look up at Coach Hart. She felt like, in some way, she knew him all along. More than that, she felt like she knew *herself*, after all.

A small sigh fell out of Mrs. Cook's lips, and she looked to the others. "Are there any more questions for Ms. Houston?" she asked.

They shook their heads, smiling politely. In all likelihood, Greta bombed the whole thing. Maybe she'd be piecing together emails to the principals from various Chicago Public Schools high schools. But at least she'd take away one thing. She could handle middle school. Especially if it came with a cute phys. ed. teacher.

"Great. And how about you? Do you have any questions for us?" Mrs. Cook lifted her eyebrows to Greta.

"Actually, yes. Just one." Bolder now, Greta met the gaze of each interviewer, landing finally on the window behind them and the neat row of little old farmhouses that sat across the street from the school. "If everything works out, I will need to find a permanent residence. I'm staying with Maggie right now, you see. So, my question is: where can I find teacher housing?"

Chapter 8—Luke

After she left, he whipped his head to Mrs. Cook. "Impressive."

"Hah!" Ms. O'Neal snorted. "She doesn't know what she wants. She might leave you high and dry after a year! I vote no."

"Hey, now," Luke reasoned, "You never know what might happen in a year."

"Plus, she's your only other applicant." Ms. Randall heaved a sigh and offered an apologetic shrug. "It's either Greta or the woman who hates where she teaches now."

Mrs. Cook studied the resumes and her notes, quiet for a minute. Finally, she looked up at the group. "I *liked* Greta. I liked her much better, actually. But the truth is, she's young. What you didn't hear her say was that she's hesitating because she wants to marry and have children, and where is the dating pool in Hickory Grove? It's the issue with any younger candidate." If Luke didn't know any better, he'd say Mrs. Cook glanced briefly, but poignantly, at him.

As she said it, the other three sets of eyes slowly turned toward Luke. His skin started to grow hot again, but more out of disappointment than the embarrassment from their obvious suggestion. He set his jaw, folded his hands over Miss Houston's resume, and stared back at each one in turn. "I can testify to the lack of a dating scene. But that's what Louisville is for. It's not far. Not for someone dead set on finding her perfect match." He pushed away from the table and leaned back into his chair. "Your option is either a woman with a track record of job dissatisfaction *or* a woman who just wants to find the best spot for herself."

"Same thing," Ms. O'Neal croaked.

"True," Luke went on, "but couldn't you sense it? The first lady—I can't even remember her name, now—she came in, tossed her bag down, spat out her answers and spent most of her time on that miserable tale of how her kids had to sit through a doggone *sex* scene *in her classroom*! Then there was Greta, who was a little nervous. Genuine. She had all the right answers, really, if you were listening. And besides, she's *from* here. You don't get more settled than that." He threw up his hands, stunned there was even a discussion. The choice was clear.

Mrs. Cook murmured in agreement, but the sigh to follow revealed that reservations lingered in her head. "We have a little time. Maybe we should give a day or two to see if new applicants come forth? I'd hate to jump the gun."

No one could accuse Danielle Cook of impatience. It was the trait that fortified her in running a school of sweaty preteens, each with a penchant for plagiarizing papers and ganging up on the weaklings among them. She was good.

But she was wrong. Luke shook his head. "What's that expression? A bird in the hand, or something?"

He tried to make eye contact with Ms. Randall. If he could get her on his side, they'd make it happen.

But Ms. Randall had already moved on, her phone out. A message from her fiancé, no doubt, pulling her attention miles and miles away from any silly interview committee.

Ms. O'Neal sniffed, took a sip from her water bottle then passed her notes to Mrs. Cook, irritated or indifferent. Both, probably. The exact opposite of how any one of them should be acting currently.

"Mrs. Crabapple?" The principal directed her attention to the quiet, rotund woman at the far end.

Mrs. Crabapple finished a notation then adjusted her eyeglasses and looked up. "Well, didn't you hear the young lady?"

Luke frowned. Mrs. Cook lifted her eyebrows, expectant.

The older woman cleared her throat. "She asked about teacher housing. How can you find an ounce of fault with her commitment? You could wait a day, sure. And in that day, your best candidate might slip right through your fingers. She's obviously looking for a placement. We have one. She has family here. So, what if she doesn't stay past a school year? One year with a great teacher surely won't *hurt*, no matter what buzzwords they throw at us. *Turnover* this and *vertical alignment* that. When I was in school, I had one year with a substitute. That's all we got. Just the one year. It was the year I decided to become a teacher. Hire her and be done. Like Luke said, a bird in the hand is worth two in the bush." She set her pencil down and tucked her hands beneath her bosom, resting them comfortably on her soft belly.

Luke could have kissed the woman. There was a reason he'd always liked Mrs. Crabapple. Her wisdom alone helped her stand out. Wisdom *and* affability.

The principal nodded her head slowly, taking in the wisdom from the old guard and pairing it neatly with Luke's more urgent plea. He was grateful the women maintained professionalism and restrained themselves for calling him out for what he was. A man with a brand-new crush. Anyway, he needed to put out that crush like a lit match that was growing too close to his skin... after all, she was with that man from Mally's, right? But Greta *did* seem like the perfect fit for the school.

And as Luke knew all too well, better teachers school wide made everyone's job easier. They'd be crazy not to lock her down, if only for a semester, much less a whole school year. Greta seemed like the type who could really elevate Hickory Grove Middle School. And it wouldn't hurt to finally work alongside someone closer in age to himself.

"All good advice. Okay. Let me take your notes and mine to the district. We'll run a background check and call her references. Let's see if this falls into place. In the meanwhile, I'm leaving the posting up."

The four women nodded and began chatting amongst themselves, throwing quick glances to Luke, who checked his phone after shuffling his pages to Mrs. Cook.

"Luke," she said as she accepted the notes and tapped them into a neat stack.

"Yes, ma'am?"

"I agree with you, really. Greta had perfect answers, for the most part. She's clearly committed. And she's very personable. Kids would love her. I just like to make sure we are thinking big picture, you know?"

He flinched at her words, defensive of the beautiful stranger. Realizing he'd better cool his jets or else be called out, he shook his head. "I know, Mrs. Cook. She may not stick around. I just think that's going to be true of anyone, young or old, married or single." He stood and shoved his hands into his pockets, rocking back on his heels.

"Well, all that said, I'm hopeful. I firmly believe she *would* make a perfect match." Mrs. Cook dipped her chin meaningfully, a bizarre grin spreading her thin lips across her face.

Luke's face reddened and he turned to leave, but Mrs. Cook cleared her throat. "One more thing, everyone."

The small group fell silent.

"Ms. Houston made a good point in her final question. It would be wise for us to collect information on local rentals or even, perhaps, put a bug in Gary Hart's ear. If we court a great candidate, we want to offer her the world, right?"

Luke nodded, but deep down something churned in him that he'd been fighting against for years. A sickening feeling in his gut that streaked through him, spinning against his gut instinct. The gut instinct that told him to stick it out for Liesel. For Mamaw's memory. For the football program and his athletes. For... a beautiful stranger?

Hah. It had been so long since Luke had been on a date, that he wasn't quite sure he even knew what beauty looked like anymore. Now, leaving the school, he felt ridiculous fighting so hard for Greta Houston with her springy blonde hair and bright blue eyes. Her full lips and perfect voice and all those big words that rolled off her tongue like she'd gone to Harvard or something. He shook his head and kicked at a rock in the middle of the sidewalk.

Luke was lonely. *Too* lonely. He'd already signed his contract for the upcoming school year, but maybe sticking around Hickory Grove wasn't such a good idea after all.

Maybe Mamaw's death didn't mean he had to stay. Maybe her death could release him from the ache in his heart. From the town with farm hands for P.E. students and vanilla malts instead of flavored lattes.

***

"I don't mean an entire reno*vation*," Liesel droned on as Luke followed her for what was fast becoming a weekly walk-through. The situation with The Hickory Grove Inn was restless. They needed a long-term plan for success, or else they'd have to sell. Likely, their very own distant relatives would involve themselves, wreaking havoc on the whole matter.

Luke blew out a sigh. "You think it needs an update?" He ran a hand along the chair rail in one of the several available guest rooms. They hadn't hung the wooden *No* on their *(No) Vacancy* sign in months. And Mamaw probably hadn't used it much herself. Of course, the poor old woman hadn't let the place fall into disrepair. None of them had, actually.

But the rooms were plain. Not quaint, Amish plain, either. Plainly dated. As though decor efforts began in the 1950s and petered just as they were getting to the matching lamps. Narrow beds, not-quite twin sized and not-quite double (Mamaw had hand sewn and quilted all of the bedding for the entire bed-and-breakfast) stood with their waxed wooden headboards centered perfectly along the wall. One dresser sat opposite, its drawers creaky and prone to derailing from their tracks. Norman Rockwell paintings hung in each room, the only semblance of an attempt to add art or style. A good one, though. Luke loved the artist. It reminded him of his childhood, when they visited for Christmas and those paintings hung in Mamaw's house instead of the guest rooms.

The rooms weren't chintzy. More, well, practical. Homemade but high quality, just how southerners liked to live, amongst the things they made with their own two hands. It meant there was a distinct lack of plastic and polyester, and that wasn't a bad thing. Still, the entire bed-and-breakfast seemed cramped, despite the scarcity of junk, and not quite in an eclectic, homey way. Instead, the place reminded him of Mamaw's little house next door, which stood as a tribute to those who survived the Great Depression. Those who collected and saved. Those who wasted not and yet wanted still.

Everything in there was heavy lace and varying shades of cream tapestry and lots and lots of crocheted blankets and quilts. They had bedding for days. They didn't need it, though, because Mamaw had seen to it that the Inn was properly outfitted. White porcelain dishes and bakeware rose in craggy towers inside small cupboards. Mamaw's good china was displayed with pride along wooden shelves that framed the breakfast nook.

Perhaps, Luke considered, it would be easy to rent out the house. It was a good size, and they might be okay with leaving some of the furniture. But Luke and Liesel first needed to ensure the Inn was sustainable. With no strong income there, they had a decision to make about what stayed in their names and what needed liquidating. Hopefully, (and deep down, Luke *was* hopeful), things could remain status quo. A little touching up. Sprucing up. Paint. An overnight manager, voila. Enough money to keep the properties running until Liesel had more time or Luke had more money or whatever.

The biggest issue with the Inn, at the present time, was that no one really wanted a room with a single bed. A single, *almost-twin-sized* bed. Plus, the place could use cohesion and charm. Though how the two could coexist escaped Luke.

Anyway, Liesel had no money to do that. Nor did Luke. And the Inn itself was obviously not a cash cow.

"Updates, yes," Liesel agreed. "By the way, do you have any leads on an overnight manager?"

Swallowing, Luke averted his gaze and shook his head. "Let's just put up a sign. It'll attract people who need a place to stay, too. I can hang a flier in the teachers' lounge. Once school starts. Or even sooner... Could be someone there looking for a rental, or something. I don't know." He was rambling.

Stepping toward the open door, she waited for him, cocking her head. Liesel could read Luke like a children's book. In one blink, she figured him out.

"Okay, who is she?"

He balked, squeezing past her into the narrow, wooden hallway. Everything in The Hickory Grove Inn was wooden. Wood. Wood. Wood. That probably should have made more sense to him, but Luke couldn't see past the dark browns and into financial stability. And with Liesel pinning him to some sort of conspiracy, the darkness swallowed him.

More than that, he felt entirely uncomfortable arranging for an overnight manager. No matter who it would be. "No one. What do you mean?" He played dumb, testing the newel post on his way down the also-narrow, also-wooden staircase.

Stella was at the front desk, leafing through an old magazine and sucking the life out of the place.

"Mmhm," his aunt chirped behind him. A cringe curled his spine at the thought of Liesel Hart, a borderline *nun,* entering his romantic business with any form of an opinion.

"What do we even sell in here?" Luke gestured to the tiny gift shop that spanned the square footage of a broom closet.

"Essentials. Snow globes. Shot glasses. Decks of cards." She walked past him into the dining room, gesturing for him to follow as she poured two mugs of coffee and set them at a little round table, a yellowing doily acting as an incomplete centerpiece.

The Hickory Grove Inn had become a bed-and-breakfast years back, when travel through Hickory Grove was nothing more than a wrong turn. It never enjoyed the traffic of a boom town or a tourist destination.

Over the years, even as people came to town for other reasons than as a mistake, the types of guests grew into a steady pattern. Family of those who lived in town but who weren't quite close enough to offer a sofa. Or those who'd flown into Louisville on their way elsewhere, destined for a bigger, brighter, better locale but too tired, after all, to drive much farther into Indiana. *Just one night here, honey. Then we can start fresh tomorrow*, the fathers would say to the mothers. Lastly, and more rarely, sometimes a couple or a small group would spend the whole day at the Horseshoe Casino on the Ohio River. If they weren't from around the area, they might get turned around and head into Hickory Grove instead of Louisville. With no motel on the map, it would become clear they'd better pull into the corner market or Mally's and ask for a little help. At that point, southerners being what they were, the owners would redirect the lost souls down the road to The Hickory Grove Inn. Always charmed by the hidden gem (as one internet user wrote of the place in an errant Facebook review), those were the ones that kept Mamaw going after Grandad's passing.

Even with the latter type of guest, the Inn looked exactly like what it was used for. Like a place with a purpose. Solid. Trustworthy. Would it ever be more? Would there ever come a day where Hickory Grove transcended the label of sleepy small farming town?

That would take a miracle. Or another casino. Or, maybe, something else that Luke and Liesel couldn't even fathom. The best they could hope for was to do their own bit of modernizing. Just so long as they kept the southern charm and the sherry, things could improve for the place. At least, that was the hope. Maybe the town didn't have to draw people in with bright lights and flashing signs. Maybe wooden bed-and-breakfasts could be enough.

"Luke." Liesel lowered her coffee, cradling it against her petite hands.

"Yes?"

"No one drives by here on a whim. Anyone looking for a house to buy or rent stays to the northeast side of town where there's new construction and family neighborhoods. The west side is all old farms and big Victorians. Why do you think a sign would help? We need to put another ad in the paper. Or maybe you can finagle something on your social media. A post or whatnot. I can write it up if you'd like?"

Sipping from his mug, he mulled it over then swallowed the hot liquid. Afternoon caffeine was never a good decision. And neither was sharing news that didn't belong to him. News that might not even be true come morning. "I have a confession."

She dropped her chin and eyed him. "Is it your friend again? Is that who's interested in renting the house?"

"Who, Mark?" Luke's mouth turned up in a crooked smile at his aunt's suspicion. So, she *didn't* suspect he had his eyes on someone. Her interest was entirely for herself, not his love life.

For once. "No. But now that you mention it, maybe he'd enjoy cuddling under an afghan with an antenna TV glowing in the dark."

It was meant to be a suggestive push. A coy reply. Mark and Liesel would make a terrible couple, but Luke never planned to give up hope. Instead, though, his words sliced through the air like a mean joke at Mamaw's expense. He dropped his gaze and shook his head. "I don't mean to make fun. I just—"

Liesel sighed, her breath rattling out from her thin lips. "I know. It's still so hard, i'n't it? Golly, Luke, if it's that big of a stressor, I could take over on nights. It's not fair to you. You have the school and your football. I'll get over her... her *stuff*. All we left were the basics, right? I won't even notice. I can handle it."

Luke covered her hand with his. He knew that Liesel could not bear to stay the night in her dead mother's house. He knew it. He wouldn't put that on his aunt, no way, no how.

Reading his mind, she squeezed Luke's hand. "I'll stay in one of the guest rooms. How about that?"

"Aunt Liesel," he replied, "I am not making you sleep on one of those tiny beds in a tiny room without so much as a coffee maker. You'd be better off moving into the rectory with Father Van. Come on, now."

After a small laugh, she released her grip and slid her hand back to the steaming mug, drawing it to her mouth for a long sip. "Then tell me. If it isn't Mark, who do you have in mind? Because I saw that wobble in your step. The stutter in your speech. Who's crawled up into that brain of yours? Who do *you* want living in Mamaw's house? Do you have an *innkeeper* in mind?"

Chapter 9—Greta

Greta pulled a fresh fitted sheet from the wicker laundry basket. Doing the wash was hardly a chore for her. She loved its rhythm, especially with the added pleasure of hanging everything out on the line. Load, wait, hang. Load, wait, hang. Fold, fold, fold. And the smell of it! Maggie had recently planted great, bushy lavender plants at the edges of the clothesline. Their blossoms sweetened the fabric better than any softener or dryer sheets.

After running a hand to smooth a few wrinkles, she plucked the flat sheet from the basket, gripped the edges, and threw it out over the bed. The soft cotton billowed up above the futon for a blissful moment. Notes of lavender hung in the air, and after a quick snap of the wrists, it lay almost perfectly in place.

She busied herself with tucking the corners and folding back the top, then adding her quilt and pillows, the ones with pretty embroidery. Maggie mentioned they were hand-me-downs from her aunt, who was a seamstress. At that, Greta's interest tripled. Gretchen joined in the conversation then, even helping Greta unpin her clothes from the line. They chatted coolly, making barely comfortable small talk.

The topics stayed superficial. Gretchen tentatively poked around about Greta's interview from the day before. Greta confessed airily that it didn't go as well as she'd have hoped.

In reply to the confession, Greta told Gretchen that what she needed was a cozy night in with a good book. Gretchen offered one of her murder mysteries. Grateful for the bit of sympathy, Greta was still hesitant to accept at first.

"I normally read..." she started to ramble off a list of literary titles, highbrow works with bizarre prose and hot-and-cold critical acclaim. Instead, she nodded. "Actually, that sounds perfect right about now."

Gretchen nearly sprinted through the field and upstairs to her bedroom before sprinting back out, her breath heavy as the thick, humid July air. "Here. I've read this one about eight times." She slapped a weathered paperback onto Greta's hand.

Accepting the book was less about the book and more about a delicate truce. Greta grinned broadly. "Thanks, Gretch. I'll read it tonight."

And she would. They parted ways after a promise to dish over fan theories in the morning before Gretchen had to leave for work.

It was just before five (the family shared an early pizza dinner), and Greta knew that getting under fresh sheets with a fast-paced mystery so early in the evening was a fool's errand. No doubt she'd fall asleep after a marathon reading session only to wake at some odd hour of the very late night, confused about the time. Anyway, Greta ought to be filling out applications. Looking for apartments in downtown Chicago, close to public transit. After all, with no immediate reaction to her interview, and a disappointing lack of contact in the past twenty-four hours, she needed to put Hickory Grove Middle and its handsome P.E. teacher firmly out of her mind.

She'd barely turned from page one to page two when her phone buzzed on the wooden crate nightstand beside her.

An unfamiliar, local number flashed on the screen, each digit a foreign object. *Could it be?*

Carefully closing her book, she took up the device. One beat later, she pressed *Accept*.

***

The call was brief and shocking, and it was quite possibly the *best* phone call she'd ever had in her whole career. It beat out every other job offer, and not because of the salary or the details of the contract.

After calling Rhett and sharing the good news (and the admission that, *yes*, she was staying in town), she did the same with Maggie. But it couldn't stop there. She had to celebrate. So, illogically, she texted Gretchen.

Now they were sitting crisscross applesauce on the futon, a bowl of popcorn between them. The last time Greta had a sleepover was in high school. With her old friend Bridget. Bridget was still, technically, Greta's best friend. But she was married with kids far away. Greta could use a little nostalgia. Mostly, she could use a little friendship.

Age difference be darned, *the Grets*, as Rhett had started calling them, had officially warmed to each other.

Greta had already spilled how she got the job and felt a weird sense of excitement.

"So, you're staying in Hickory Grove, obviously?" Gretchen asked, munching away.

Greta shrugged. "Yes?" It came out more like a question than a statement. "I'm looking for a rental, but in all these years, no one has erected an apartment complex. I mean there's Hickory Hall, but that doesn't count.

Gretchen made a face. "No, don't live there."

"I saw a string of condos just north of town when I was driving around after the interview yesterday. Up past the school? Do you know what I'm talking about?"

"Greta," Gretchen rested a hand on her arm, "you don't have to move. Okay? This barn is, like, *perfect* for you. I have a room in the farmhouse. And soon enough, I'll probably get my own place somewhere else."

"No. Come on, Gretch. You're young. You're saving money. You belong *here*." Greta pushed a finger into the top of the quilt. "I'll be out soon, and you'll have your futon and a sewing machine that works." Both women glanced at the wooden sewing table on the far side of the space. An antique Singer growing dust. Several parts were missing. Neither Gretchen nor Maggie could find them.

A shallow sigh escaped Gretchen's lips, and she turned her head back to Greta. "I have to admit, I like you being here." A small smile turned her lips up.

Greta smiled back. "I like being here, too. But this is your home. I'll find my own, then I'll come back here and read one of your books while you sit over there and hum along to a pretty pattern."

Brightness washed over Gretchen's face, and she flopped back on the bed. "Okay, fine. So, anyways, tell me more about the interview. Was old Ms. O'Neal there?"

Smugly, Greta lifted an eyebrow. "Ah, so my impression wasn't totally off."

"Ugh, she was *awful*. It's like she saw the worst in you and dragged it out for a fight or something. She's probably the reason I didn't get a scholarship."

Rolling her eyes at Gretchen's dramatics, Greta replied, "I couldn't get a read on Crabapple. Did you have her too? She was friendly looking but quiet."

"Hmm, I think she was at the high school when I was in middle school. Then she switched when I promoted. I never really knew her."

Greta plucked a few kernels from the bowl and jiggled them in her hand like loose change. Should she dare to ask about the coach? No. It would undermine everything. It would look like the *only* reason Greta was staying in town was because of some hot teacher. And that just wasn't true. She didn't even know the guy. All she knew was that Mrs. Cook said everything she needed to hear. Classroom autonomy. Administrative support. Fair compensation. And, as the woman added, they were *actively seeking local housing arrangements. A stipend might be available.* Greta was set. The handsome jock was just icing on the cake. Anyway, he could have a girlfriend! He could be one of those guys who was married but couldn't wear a ring. Maybe he was allergic to precious metals. Anyway, he was just a guy. Greta was there for the job. The kids.

"Did you have a teacher named Coach Hart? For P.E.?" It fell out of her mouth before she could swallow the words back down.

Gretchen's head snapped left, and she scrambled back to a sitting position. Her eyes grew wide. "Coach *Hart*? Was in the interview?"

Splotches of red instantly bloomed across Greta's chest, climbing like footprints up her neck and settling on her cheeks. She could feel them. "Yes?" again, her voice rose up, turning one syllable into two, two trembled beats. Like a poet who took a simple declarative sentence and morphed into a new word. Ye-es. He *was* there, wasn't he? His last name *was* Hart, wasn't it? Gretchen's question emitted like a bullet from a gun. "Should he not have been?" Greta added, eyeing the girl, who pressed her hands to her knees and leaned into Greta.

"I have no idea. I guess P.E. teachers can be on interview committees, but..."

"But what?" Greta frowned at Gretchen, but a small smile formed on her lips.

"He's, like, he's really attractive. And he's probably *your* age."

My age, Greta thought. What was that supposed to mean? The point was a harsh reminder that Gretchen really was much younger. "Did you have a crush on him?"

"Ew," Gretchen replied instantly. "Not *then*. Not when I was in middle school."

Greta simply lifted her eyebrows and waited.

Sure enough, Gretchen shook her head and rolled her eyes. "He's also the high school football coach. And he comes into Mally's all the time."

A picture was forming in Greta's mind. Coach Hart wasn't just a handsome *man*. He was *that* teacher. The one the girls giggled about. The one who probably bore a little local fame. And the football coach, too? The whole fantasy began to morph into little more than a high school daydream. Not her style. Greta Houston was a student of literature. An educator of children. She cleaned her house (or wherever she was living) and read books in her spare time. Waving pom poms from a sideline every Friday night as rowdy teens splashed soda in the stadium wasn't exactly her idea of a good time.

The whole conversation with Gretchen was actually freeing. It freed Greta to focus on the one thing she *wanted* to focus on so long as she was in town. Her career. She could get back in touch with Bridget, maybe. They could meet for weekend girls' nights in downtown Louisville. Maybe Maggie would go sometimes. Maybe, if Greta was still single by then, she'd take Gretchen to a classy wine bar for her twenty-first birthday and casually bump into some banking executive.

Dating a football coach in her hometown was the exact *opposite* of what Greta hoped to accomplish in life. Case closed.

Gretchen, after trying unsuccessfully to rile Greta up about the coach, finally rose to leave, the half-empty popcorn bowl clutched in front of her. "Tomorrow afternoon is the Fish Fry at Little Flock. I'm going to bring Theo. Do you think you can come?"

Chapter 10—Luke

He'd politely informed Liesel that, no, he did not have an *innkeeper* in mind.

Then, later, he got the text from Mrs. Cook. She'd sent it to all of the members of the interview committee. *Greta Houston is signing on. Thanks for helping make H.G.M.S. great!*

When Luke opened the message, he was standing outside of the parish hall with an apron tied across his torso. It read *Don't Hassle the Cook*, and Luke pointed to the grease-stained letters any time someone so much as approached him, then cracked up and asked how he could help.

As the words of the text glared up from his phone screen, he stopped clacking the slippery tongs, nearly dropping them into the deep fryer.

Little Flock hosted an outdoor fish fry every other Friday from Memorial Day way up until Labor Day. Then again come Lent, but those were indoors.

Some weeks were busier and more celebratory than others, and this one was sure to be a blow out. It was the last Little Flock Fry-day, as locals called it, before teachers reported back to school to set up their classrooms and sit in professional development training sessions. The last one before students would finally clean out their backpacks from the end of the past school year. They'd head into Louisville and shop for a week's worth of new clothes, returning home to hang them up with the tags still on.

It was Luke's favorite time of summer because football was now also in full swing. Busy was good. Busy was welcome.

It would distract him from the strange stress of the bed-and-breakfast, anyway.

Fry-days were keeping him sane, though. He liked juggling evening practice with the obligation to cook for upwards of one hundred folks, forty of them being his own famished football players who usually turned up for the cook-out.

That evening, Luke oversaw the fish. Liesel tended to white rice, beverages, and desserts. Meanwhile, Father Van stood in his street clothes by the grill. Corn on the cob roasted in front of him. Five round folding tables dotted the grass, only two with umbrellas. The other three enjoyed fortunate positions beneath green-leaved oak trees, broad and shady. For a modest, local church event, it was always neatly appointed. With one look at the set-up, you'd know exactly why Liesel Hart didn't have much time to take on The Hickory Grove Inn. She threw her all into Little Flock.

A cracking voice dragged Luke's attention away from his phone screen. "Coach!"

Snapping back to life, he focused on the boy who appeared, stretching out a paper plate, ready to get his grub on.

"Ky Engel! How are ya, kiddo?" Luke clamped down on a thick patty and plopped it on the boy's plate. The kid started rambling about how he wanted to be the water boy for the upcoming season. That's when something dawned on Luke.

"Ky *Engel*," he repeated half under his breath once Ky had finished his case for getting the job.

"Yessir?" Eager and tubby, Ky wasn't always Luke's best student, but he was loyal to Luke, and he loved football.

"Is your mama here, Ky?"

It must have given the boy the wrong impression because Ky's eyes lit up in excitement. He whipped his head around and shielded his eyes from the sinking sunlight. "There, Coach Hart!" Ky jabbed a chunky white finger at a small group walking up the hill from the parking lot. "I ran ahead, but she's coming. Look!"

Luke raised his hand and squinted into the sun. He could make out the redhead in front. Maggie. Ky's mom. To her side and *holding her hand* was the man Luke had taken for Greta's boyfriend at Mally's.

He wasn't, though. He was with Maggie Engel. Clear as day.

Luke's chest tightened and he looked past Maggie and the familiar man to Ky's older sister and her boyfriend. Gretchen and Theo. Luke had taught Gretchen in school, but he came to know Theo from his hanging around the diner every time Luke happened to go in for a coffee or a sandwich. He was more of a regular than any local in town, despite the fact that he wasn't even from Hickory Grove.

Another figure, smaller and light-footed in a flowery sundress strode behind.

Mrs. Cook's newest hire. The woman who would make H.G.M.S. *great!* Greta.

And she was *alone*.

"Ky," Luke said. The boy whipped around again, his light hair hanging in his eyes like a mop. *Wasn't his mama a hairdresser?* "I'll make you a deal." He lowered his voice and gave the kid a conspiratorial look. Ky leaned in. "You can be this season's water boy..."

"Uh huh?" Ky whispered back, his face as serious as a Catholic at confession.

"*If,*" Luke went on, emphasizing each word with careful diligence, "you can tell me about your new family friend." He jutted his chin to the group who now lingered at the drink coolers on the far side, by the shaded tables.

Ky scrunched up his face momentarily, then the lightbulb hit. "Miss Greta!" His voice all but echoed around the field, bouncing off Luke and the deep fryer then behind and toward the tables.

Luke cringed and peeked out of one eye. Sure enough, she heard. Even worse, Ky was running—faster than he'd ever run in P.E. class—directly for the now-petrified-looking blonde.

Muttering a barnyard swear under his breath, Luke wiped his forehead with the back of his hand and glanced left, toward where Father Van stood, greeting a line of other newcomers.

Liesel emerged from the parish hall, chatting sweetly with Fern Gale, one of the women from her Ladies Auxiliary. They brushed past him and set out pitchers of freshly squeezed lemonade on each table. Earlier, right when Luke arrived to help set up, Fern and Liesel had scurried off, all hushed voices and girlhood giggles. He was happy Liesel had found a good friend in Fern but uninterested in the older women's banter. Now, he was desperate for it. If *only* they'd stop and chat with him. Make him look occupied and innocent and unrelated to Ky's screech.

Again, wiping his forehead, Luke forced himself to focus on serving one of his player's family as they made their way down the line toward him. They exchanged a few comments about the young man's promise for the season. Luke suggested there might be a starting position if the kid put in a little extra time on the field, and a knowing look passed between the parents. Luke caught the flicker between them. The shared needs and wants. The shared hopes.

"Here she is!"

Just as the family shuffled off to gather their plastic utensils on the next table, Ky reappeared a few feet off. He was dragging Greta behind him.

Backlit by the sun, Greta glowed as she let Ky pull her up to Luke. Everything about her seemed at once new and entirely unfamiliar. She was the same woman who sat near him at Mrs. Cook's interview table. Now, though, her hair fell a little looser. The light in her eyes took on a twinkle. A sundress swayed just above her knees, and pink toes poked out from strappy sandals. Finally, and most notably, her mouth spread in a wide smile, white teeth flashing behind glossy lips.

He started to shake his head and glare at Ky, but it was too late now. Ky was going on and on about how Miss Greta—*Miss Houston*—was going to be a new teacher at *their* school, and she also happened to live with him, and she was super-duper cool and nice, and Luke would *definitely* like working with her.

That's when Luke, discreetly as possible, swiped his hand like a blade across the side of his neck, willing Ky to get a clue. "Okay, Ky. Thank you for the introduction." He chuckled half-heartedly and tried to pinch his shoulders up as if to say, *Kids these days!*

Greta lifted an eyebrow to match her smile-turned-smirk. "Coach Hart, right?"

After gulping, all he could do was nod for the moment. Then, humiliatingly, he managed to lift his tongs and a paper plate and say, "Fried catfish?"

She laughed. A full-bellied laugh that bent her at the waist and turned Ky's innocent game plan into a coming of age moment. Luke felt like he, too, was coming of age just then. He couldn't quite recall the last time he'd been so taken by a woman. Years. Truly. If ever.

"What is it you wanted to talk to me about, Coach?" She clasped her hands behind her back and glanced around now.

Luke moaned inwardly then raised his eyebrows to Ky, waiting for the boy to fess up.

Ky opened his mouth to answer on Luke's behalf, and they both turned to him, equally expectant. "Well," Ky began, returning to his innocence and launching into the terms of the deal he and Luke had just agreed upon moments before.

"I didn't exactly..." Luke set the tongs down and rounded his little table, squeezing the boy's shoulders with his plastic-glove-wrapped hands. He gave Greta a look, but her expression turned skeptical.

Luke stood at a crossroads: either tell the truth and declare that he did not want to talk *to* Greta—that he just asked Ky about her and the kid took it too far. Or Luke could cover for both of them. "I just wanted to say... I was just wondering..." Luke shook his head. He was at a total loss. There was no pretending that he didn't want to talk to her. He'd better come up with something—*anything*—fast.

"Is this her?"

The question came from behind Greta, its syllables crisp and high pitched and painfully, clearly referring to the beautiful blonde standing squarely in between them.

Luke stared daggers at his aunt.

Greta and Ky turned to see her. Greta's expression became wary, and she looked back at Luke, the beginnings of a frown curling her mouth.

It was a long shot, but Luke had a gut feeling about where Liesel might go. He took a stab. "You mean for the Inn; right, Aunt Liesel?" Luke pinned her with a look. *Play along, please.*

Greta's frown deepened, but the flicker in her eye fell away. Her budding discomfort turned to straight confusion, which was far preferable. Luke, too, was growing uncomfortable. But now he and his aunt joined in on a plan. A saving grace. Something to say to take the heat off his apparent and entirely inappropriate crush.

Liesel's eyebrows shot up, and she answered, "Right. Our new innkeeper? You, my dear, must be the young lady looking for accommodations in town." His aunt passed a hand toward Fern Gale, who nodded as though in the loop.

Now it was Luke's turn to frown. He shed his gloves and set them on his table, propping his hands on his hips in order to fully address the matter. The awkward, beautiful matter. The perfect scenario. It was working. He was free from humiliation. Maybe.

Fern pressed her lips into a thin smile and nodded gravely. "Maggie told me all about you, Greta. Welcome back to Hickory Grove, hun." The woman spread her arms, and Greta stepped into the hug. Bewilderment slipped from her face, in its place a new smile. Easier. Softer.

"Fern? Fern *Monroe*?"

"The one and only, sweet pie."

"You look darn near the exact same as you did when I was a little girl." Greta's eyes grew wide as she studied the woman. "It's nice to see you... *out*. And about!" A smile flashed across Greta's face.

Fern had something of a reputation in town. Since she was young, she'd been a shut-in. A recluse. Recently, she reemerged into society, taking baby steps to do more than scurry in and out of mass on Sundays. She'd become more comfortable, it seemed, and showed up at various events around town. In fact, Luke had met her through Little Flock. It was no wonder Greta knew her, too.

"So, let me get this straight. Rhett and Maggie told you, Fern, about my predicament. You told...?" The question hung in the air, and Luke rushed to answer it.

"My aunt. This is my Aunt Liesel."

Liesel squeezed Greta's fingertips. "Charmed, darlin', but we met years back. Here at Little Flock. You and your brother, Rhett, were just babies back then. I was ahead in school by some years." Liesel pushed the pads of her fingertips beneath her eyes.

Greta nodded, appearing to take in all the news at once. "Right." She inhaled sharply and glanced at Ky then Luke. Then back at Liesel. "So, you mentioned an *inn*? You're not referring to..."

"The Hickory Grove Inn, yes." Liesel took a sip of her lemonade and raised her eyebrows over the rim at Luke.

"You know it, I'm sure." Fern added.

Greta blinked. "Of course. Just up the hill." She gestured behind her. "You're... you're selling it?"

"Oh no, honey," Liesel replied. "Wouldn't dream of that. Luke's mamaw just passed. My mother. She lived in the cottage next door. Maybe you heard about the services? Anyway, her house was that precious two-story Victorian. You know the one, no doubt."

"Victorian? No," Fern interrupted. "I'd say it's got that, you know, Cape Cod style? The shutters and the beige clapboard and white trim and whatnot."

"I always thought it was more farmhouse, actually," Luke interjected, then felt silly. He'd been part owner of the bed-and-breakfast for just weeks and now all of a sudden, he was some expert in housing design? Ha. He shook his head and held up a hand. "We've been advertising for a manager's position. A night manager."

Fern went on, taking a step forward and nearly cutting Luke off from a view of Greta. "You see, Greta, when Maggie told me that you had your sights set on finding a place, I told her to tell you that you could rent a room from *me*." Luke threw a sidelong glance at Fern. It wasn't so farfetched. She lived in a mansion on Pine Tree Lane and probably had the space. Still...

"Oh?" Greta's smile grew thin.

"Yes, but Maggie insisted you'd either stay in her barn or find your own place. At Ladies Auxiliary this morning, I relayed the matter to Liesel, who shared with me her own problem."

"Which is?" Greta flicked a glance to Luke, and he could see plain as day she wasn't quite keeping up with it. His off-the-cuff plan to just launch into an offer of taking on the overnight duty would have been *way* clearer.

He cleared his throat. "Maybe I could just explain this?" It came out with a squeak, and both Liesel and Fern hushed him on the spot, his aunt glaring at him meaningfully. Maybe *he* was the confused one.

"Sweetheart," Fern slipped her arm through Greta's as though she were confiding in a dear friend. "That little cottage that Mamaw Hart left behind is vacant and in want of a tenant. Now, the nice thing is the rent is very, *very* reasonable." Fern turned to Liesel, "Right, Liesel?"

Liesel nodded and jumped in. "We'll practically pay *you* to live there." Liesel turned to Luke, a domino effect of assurances. "Right, Luke?"

He rubbed the back of his neck and shook his head. It was clear now that the two women were scheming, and he was very worried that they were about to ruin everything. "It's just a place to stay. If you're still looking. That's all I was going to tell you." He closed his eyes and swallowed, picking up his plastic gloves and ready to return to shelling out catfish patties.

Then, Greta spoke. "Um, this is a lot to take in." Her face softened again, but worry lines appeared at the corners of her eyes as she looked at the two icy southern women who were laying it on thick for a reason unknown to poor Greta. "Let me talk to my brother." She wrapped an arm around Ky's shoulders. "And Maggie. See what they think about it."

"You do that, honey," Liesel chirped back. Then, as though Luke needed *one more reason* to never talk to his aunt *ever* again, she *winked* at him. A big, fat, full-faced wink.

And much to Luke's palpable horror, Greta saw the wink, frowned, and walked Ky back to his mother and her entourage.

But that wasn't the worst part. The worst part was that he would have to face her on the following Monday. At *work*.

Luke Hart was never going to live that wink down.

The only thing he wanted to do now was get clear away from his meddling aunt. No matter how well-intentioned she and her eccentric friend, he couldn't sacrifice his love life for a family heirloom.

That's when it occurred to Luke that, actually, he didn't even have a love life.

Now it was clear that he wouldn't have one, either. Not if he stuck around Hickory Grove, Indiana with its nosy residents. Not if he committed to being Mamaw's postmortem innkeeper, either.

He grabbed the tongs, clacked them together a few times and got back to work. He had at least one more year in Hickory Grove. And he had obligations. Football. Fish frys. And getting through the school year unscathed by the enigmatic new hire who was going to make H.G.M.S. so *great!*

Chapter 11—Greta

"What was all *that* about?" Maggie asked once Greta and Ky were safely back to the table. Greta had lost her appetite during the whole ordeal, her stomach flip-flopping in confusion.

Maggie sent Rhett, Ky, and Dakota back to the line to get platefuls for the girls. Once they were gone, Greta replied, "Did you tell Miss Fern that I needed a place to stay?" She pressed the heel of her hand to her head, willing away the threat of a headache.

Shrugging, Maggie took a sip of her lemonade and picked up the Barbie that Briar had dropped. "We were just talking. That's all."

"Well, Fern told Liesel Hart. And Liesel is Luke's aunt."

"Who's Luke?" Maggie frowned.

Greta assumed Gretchen would have gossiped with her mother about their awkward conversation from before. Apparently not. "He's a P.E. teacher at the school. He was on the interview committee. He's... well, he's really hot."

"Oh, *Coach* Hart. Of course I know him. He's the high school football coach, too. He's always at the diner with another one of them teachers, a whistle around his neck and playbook sprawled out across the table. It's adorable. He's like a little old-fashioned gym teacher who moonlights on the sidelines." Maggie paused, studying Greta as though through new eyes.

The image clung to Greta's brain like syrup, dripping down and making her feel woozy and flirty. "Well, it was awkward."

"What do you mean it was awkward?" Maggie pressed, furrowing her brow. "And what does Coach Hart have to do with you needing a place?" The frown turned suspicious.

Greta let out a dramatic sigh. "Well, apparently Luke's grandmother passed away. And, if I've got this right, her house is available for rent. But it seems to come with a catch."

"That's right. June Hart. So sad. She was a good woman. So, what's the catch?" Maggie took another sip, and Greta suspected she was only drinking in order to hide her reaction.

Shrugging, Greta's face fell. "That's just it. I don't know."

***

Southern small towns being what they were, Maggie promised Greta they'd get to the bottom of the matter. Though, Greta was beginning to suspect that in all likelihood it was as simple as southern charm. A kindly neighbor—or kindly *co-worker*—who offered a well-timed opportunity.

Coincidence. No catch.

And yet, Maggie had spent the remainder of the evening flitting about the fish fry, bouncing from Father Van to Rhett and his friend Jake, landing finally among the coaches' wives.

It was a brilliant move, actually, and Greta studied her carefully. Gretchen and Theo had slipped off into the woods, which left Greta in the position of tending to little Briar. Greta could just steal the little girl away. To have a child of her own felt like a faraway dream, something that could so easily disappear on her tongue like cotton candy. The anticipation and taste were so sweet, but the reality left her wanting. Greta feared she was on the edge of the end of her opportunity, even despite modern technology and other options. For Greta to get the chance to grow her own sweet baby and raise it—her heart ached to miss the experience. It ached.

But the ache was not about to dictate her standards or her decisions. Other parts of her life did that for her. Like her career. And a place to live. Besides, everything still hung in the balance. Sure, she had a *job*, but did she have a home in Hickory Grove? A real one?

***

"I've got the scoop." Maggie lifted Briar from her white plastic chair and pulled the sleepy-eyed girl onto her lap as she slid beside Greta. Her voice was a giddy whisper, and Greta leaned in immediately, her eyes sweeping through the darkness, landing for the millionth time on Luke. Mostly, he stayed in position at the deep fryer, his attention securely on his task and distracted only when someone came up for catfish. His eyes never once flitted in her direction. It was just in the past ten minutes that he had finally left, first disappearing into the parish hall then returning outside to reign over the football players who laughed around a bonfire out past the tables in a clearing on the edge of the woods. Ky was out there, too. Even younger Dakota. They sat on the fringe, with another boy who looked to be closer to their age. Luke stood nearest them, protectively.

"What?" Greta hissed back.

"First of all, I think there *is* a catch."

Her heart sank. "Like what? Is it a dump? Is the rent super high? Did they fib or something?"

"No, no, no." Maggie licked her lips, grabbing her sweaty lemonade, the ice melted down to nothing by now. The white rim of the cup caught a reflection of the fire and bobbed with light in front of Maggie's face.

Briar swatted at a mosquito for the millionth time, and Greta reached her two hands out and slapped it between her palms. "Spill, Miss Maggie Devereux. *Spill.*"

Maggie gulped the beverage and nodded. Her face serious, her voice low but animated, she leveled her gaze on Greta and divulged every gory detail. "Okay, here we go. *So*, Liesel, bless her *heart*, can't stand to be in her dead mother's house. Who can blame her? Right? Well, Luke, bless *his* heart, is about to be too busy, what with school *and* football, to keep checking in on the old place. And you *know* how football season is around here." Maggie paused only to lift her eyebrow. "Well, you see, turns out that Mamaw Hart was basically the night manager for the inn, in addition to *running* the place. Then when she went into care, well, Stella—she's the day clerk—pitched in. But Stella is, well. Let's just say it wasn't working. Liesel helped where she could, and I guess Luke was practically on call *twenty-four-seven*. Now that ol' June Hart is dead and gone, Liesel and Luke are all but at each other's throats over what to do with the whole thing. They have the house and that precious little inn but hardly any income to justify keeping both. I mean, don't get me wrong, I doubt either one is hurting for cash, but running a second home and a literal *mansion* can't be cheap, right? But then again, it's an *heirloom*, you know, so there's *that* to consider." Maggie stopped for a breath but instead drew the red cup back to her lips, gulping at it again as though it wasn't the lemonade that could possibly quench her thirst, but finishing the gossip.

Briar started to whine. She'd hit her wall.

Greta pressed Maggie, desperate for the final details. "So then, that's it? Why did you say there *was* a catch?"

"They don't exactly want to rent the house next door. It's not meant to be a 'rental house,'" Maggie dragged her fingers into quotation marks into the night air.

"What do you mean?" Greta asked, chewing furiously on her fingernails, bitter bits of pink polish depositing on her tongue and lips. The chance at a place to live might be just out of reach. Or just within it, depending on what her friend said next.

"Greta, honey. Listen to me." Maggie's eyes flashed in the dark. Wisps of Briar's downy hair blowing up into her face. "They want to turn it into an *innkeeper's house*."

Chapter 12—Luke

Ignoring Greta for the duration of Fry-day proved dang near impossible. Luke had never focused harder on a bubbling basin of grease.

Even with concerted effort, he still couldn't shake her. Not her beauty and not the painful way she excused herself from the conversation with Liesel and Fern.

Besides that, his and Liesel's one shot at a decent candidate for the Inn blew away like dandelion fluff on a summer breeze.

The ensuing weekend saw him hitting the playbooks and tapes again, squeezing in his own workouts on the track and meeting Mark for breakfast after mass. And, of course, hours at the inn. Liesel didn't pressure him to be there, just as Mamaw never would have. But that pressure existed, pulling Luke over whenever he had a spare moment. Come Monday, when it was time to report back to school, Mamaw's house was cleaned out, and Stella was advised to call Liesel if anything came up, since Luke couldn't leave work as easily.

Liesel's stress had grown insurmountable, though. She wrung her hands and fretted to the high Heavens about whether to sell. At one point, Luke couldn't hold back any longer, telling her if she and Fern hadn't pressured Greta, she might have said yes.

Then again, he knew that was a long shot, anyway. They hadn't even spelled out the terms of the arrangement. Plus, now they'd be working together. She was too cute to make it a comfortable scenario, and Liesel was too overbearing and fraught with anxiety for anything to go well. Liesel murmured that she'd reach out to Maggie herself to set up an interview, which Luke fiercely opposed, threatening his aunt that if she meddled one more time, he would step away from the whole thing.

He hated to do that to his aunt, who really did mean well and really did have cause to panic. But Luke couldn't allow stress from his personal life to seep into his workplace.

Of course, as he stepped from the shower Monday morning, a fresh polo and khaki shorts laid out on his bed, new sneakers on the floor, he knew it already had.

Not once in Luke's entire teaching career had he laid out his outfit the night before. He suspected other types (such as Mark) took to such measures to prepare. That wasn't really Luke though. He was a casual guy. So, stepping into the carefully selected outfit felt both ridiculous and also... important.

He showed up just before seven-thirty, which is when Mrs. Cook and her admin team would have breakfast and coffee set out. Before going to the cafeteria, where their Welcome Back meeting would commence, he diverted to his office, adding an extra spray of cologne and grabbing his spare pack of gum. Plus, he had an extra clipboard and notebook on his desk, which he grabbed along with a pencil.

By the time he made it to the cafeteria, it was seven thirty-five. Standing on the freshly waxed tiles, he let out a sigh and scanned the space. Some of the staff had already arrived, and Mark was slogging down the buffet table, neatly curating his breakfast table.

No sign of Greta Houston.

Luke found an empty, outermost table, set his things down, then joined Mark in line.

"Welcome back, my man." He squeezed his friend's shoulders and grabbed a plate, scooping fresh fruit and sliding a bagel on as they made brief small talk and wandered back to the seats Luke had picked out.

"Let me grab my stuff." Mark walked to a different empty table and returned with his own clipboard and notebook as well as a novel.

Luke pointed to it. "Think you'll sneak in a little recreation?"

"Always," Mark replied with a grin.

"Another historical?" Luke tried to make out the cover, and his friend grabbed the book and held it up.

"Not this time. This one is a Mitch Albom. Lighter reading. And deeper reading, I guess. One of those books that just grabs you and sucks you in. Fast read, but it'll pull your guts out.

Luke nodded and swept his eyes across the cafeteria again.

"She's not here," Mark said through bites of a croissant.

Three members of the English department sauntered in from the door that connected to the front office. Luke tried to avoid eye contact, but Mark raised his hand and waved to them.

"What are you *doing*?" Luke hissed. He hadn't chugged enough coffee to pretend he was in the loop on their Shakespeare references and snide comments about grammar. "I'd rather sit with the maintenance guys."

"Just watch and learn," Mark replied, his voice low.

"Donna, Judy!" He smiled and waved at the open seats. The third, Susan, beelined for the breakfast spread. "Come on over. Plenty of room."

Luke mustered a smile to the women, immediately uneasy.

Thankfully, Mark took the lead. "How was your summer ladies?"

The women chatted happily about where they went and what they did. Books they read. Luke forced himself to nod along. At one point, when Susan had returned, a realization formed in Luke's mind.

He glanced around the room again, while Mark was re-counting what he'd read so far in *Tuesdays with Morrie*. When there was still no sign of Greta, he started to eye empty seats at the smattering of round tables. Three with the science people. Four with the secretary and dean. Two open spots at the table where the other social studies teacher sat with the math folks.

One at his own table. With the English teachers.

Luke slowly turned his head to Mark, who had broken from his own animated conversation about the merits of the memoir in a publishing world dominated by novels, or something.

"I know *exactly* what you're doing," he hissed.

"I'm not doing *anything*," Mark replied, his eyes flashing beyond Luke. "Now, look alive, kid." Then, abruptly he added, "Stand up."

"What?" Luke asked, frowning.

"Be a gentleman and *stand up*."

"Why?" But as he said it, Mark rose and smiled at something behind Luke.

The other women at the table turned their attention, too, and immediately oohed and ahhed and gushed.

"Good morning, everyone!" Mrs. Cook's voice rose cheerfully behind Luke. He whipped around in his seat and started to stand, only to come face to face with *her*.

Mrs. Cook pressed on. "I'd like you to meet Miss Greta Houston. She's joining our Language Arts Department this year."

The others at the table stood, and handshakes were crossing the laminate wood top, leaving in their ghostly wake invisible threads of a spider web. The H.G.M.S. tradition of warmth and welcoming was alive and well. But when Greta had finished smiling and taking in the new names, and when Mrs. Cook had left her there to go see about a sound check for her microphone, a waiting quiet wrapped them.

Luke pulled himself together and offered his hand. "Miss Houston," he said, mustering a professional tone. "Congratulations."

"Thank you," she answered. He could have sworn he detected a smile behind her lips.

It was time she took a seat. The empty one, conveniently and *in*conveniently was directly next to Luke.

He wavered momentarily, struck by the fact that he wasn't sure if now was a good time to pull a seat out for her or if it would come across as indecent. If he did, was he being respectful? The rules and nuances of the workplace momentarily eluded him, as though he was experiencing a stroke, then and there. He froze up, and instead of making a decision, he awkwardly just rested his hand on the chair back.

"Um," Greta looked around the table, but the others had returned their attention to Mark, who launched into another controversial point about the usefulness of *Spark Notes* in the modern English classroom.

Luke, still frozen, gathered the energy to swallow. He watched Greta's eyes drift down to his hand, but words stuck in his throat like gum.

"Is that seat...?" She pointed to the chair, which finally moved him to action. The only thing he could do was to pull it out.

The metal legs screeched against the tile, and all eyes were on them.

Luke murmured an apology and sank into his own wobbly chair as Greta made herself comfortable.

"You should grab a bite to eat, dear," Susan pointed out as she bit into a blueberry muffin.

Again, Luke wondered if the polite thing was to get Greta a plate, or if that would be wildly inappropriate. Never in his life had he questioned the norms of interacting with a co-worker at a work event. It was ridiculous. He closed his eyes momentarily, willing his brain to just turn off already.

"Oh, thanks," Greta replied, glancing briefly at Luke.

Silently, he took a deep breath. "I need a top-up. I'll walk with you, Miss Houston."

And like that, the switch flipped on. His brain settled into position, and he was even able to shake off the feeling of Mark's eyes on him, filled with amusement, no doubt.

"You can call me Greta, you know."

He smiled down at her. "Call me Luke."

"Right," she answered. "Gretchen told me that was your name."

His heart swung low into his stomach and bounced back up. "Gretchen?" She was talking to other people about him? Maybe a chance existed, still. He just needed to keep his mouth shut about Liesel and the Inn and the house. Play it cool. Teaching stuff. What they had in common. Those were good topics. Avoid her living arrangements and anything he might have to do with them.

"Engel? I'm staying with her family until I find a place."

He winced then glanced down at her. They stood at the coffee table, and she was pouring herself a cup and shaking her head slowly.

"Everything okay?" he asked.

"Oh, yes. I just... nothing." A small smile took shape on her lips, but he tried to look away.

"I'm going to go in for seconds, myself." He gestured to the plates and followed her down the line. They didn't speak as she added bits of fruit and a cup of yogurt to her plate, appearing to hem and haw over the croissants.

"They're delish. The cafeteria staff bakes everything *here*, which I guess is super rare for a school district."

But Greta just shook her head. "I'm not very hungry."

They returned to the table, and Luke caught Mark's stare. Luke shook his head discreetly, a warning.

"So, Miss Houston," Mark said, his voice booming. "Tell us about yourself."

Luke looked at her, waiting to hear more of what he already knew.

She surprised him, though, and instead of reviewing her qualifications and why she chose to apply and this, that, the other, she went a different direction. "Well, I was born and raised here. My brother, Rhett, and I came to H.G.M.S., although I don't think any of our teachers are still here." She looked around the room. "I left for college and studied English, of course. Mainly, I wanted to have a job that would allow me to spend lots of time with my family."

"Are you married?" Mark asked.

Luke knocked his friend's knee beneath the table. But Mark kept a straight face, and Luke realized that if there was any new information to be mined, it was best that Mark do it. So, he relaxed, leaning back, sipping his coffee, and listening.

"Oh, um. Almost," she answered.

Coffee dribbled into the wrong pipe at the back of Luke's throat, and he started to choke.

Mark gave him a thud on the back, which made it way worse momentarily. When he finally came up for air, he glanced around the table. The women were staring at him, including Greta. He began to apologize, but searing feedback echoed across the cafeteria. Mrs. Cook was at the mic, her finger to her ear and her hand outstretched as a tech guy scrambled around her to fix the problem.

Quickly, it resolved, and Mrs. Cook welcomed everyone back and opened the meeting.

And Luke had no idea what in the world Greta meant when she said *Almost*.

Chapter 13—Greta

Greta sat and listened to Mrs. Cook pep them up with a quick overview of what made H.G.M.S. *great!* Then she brought them back down to reality with humbling test data before pepping them up again over parent survey responses. Greta listened to information on the new bell schedule and professional learning community norms. She listened to the dean and the secretary review attendance and grade procedures. When to send students to the office with referrals, when to manage the behavior independently.

But Greta couldn't *hear* much. Blood pulsed through her veins, filling her head and muffling the too-loud sound system and the too-familiar droning of administrators at the start of the new year.

If she weren't sitting next to Coach Hart—*Luke*—she'd be able to concentrate. She could take notes. She could have a list of questions on hand for the next time she got the principal alone.

None of that was possible in his presence, and Greta could not tell if it was because of their awkward conversation at the fish fry or because of how her body buzzed in such close proximity to his. Her palms were sweaty. Her eyes dilated. Her flesh prickled with heat.

Plus, she hadn't meant to end the history teacher's line of questioning with a vague reference like she had done. An *almost* family? How silly. Greta felt fairly humiliated to come across as a melodramatic enigma. The first chance she had, she'd clear that up. However, the morning info session seemed to go on and on endlessly. It was impossible to focus on anything. She was too aware of Luke. Too distracted.

Not to mention, her home life was still lacking the whole *home* part. When Maggie had told her that Liesel Hart wanted someone to help run the bed-and-breakfast, she knew it was a nonstarter. She had zero hospitality experience, and besides, she was beginning a new school year at a new school in a new(ish) town. Anyway, the whole thing came across as extremely awkward, and by the end of Liesel and Fern's pitch, Luke was all but ignoring her. Clearly, he didn't want to mix business with *business*. A fellow teacher *and* a property manager were too much for one man to handle. She could tell.

Fortunately, Rhett promised he'd spend the day driving around looking for rental signs. He told Greta he'd call her with anything that looked halfway decent. She appreciated the gesture, even if she suspected her brother hadn't quite listened to her non-negotiables. At any mention of Greta's plans to find a place, he was conveniently absent. She'd begun to wonder if he was a good man for the job, but then, she wasn't picky. At least, not *very* picky.

The only property that was totally out of the question, of course, was June Hart's old home. That family's bed-and-breakfast was a better fit for someone else. A small-town girl with small-town dreams. Not Greta, who simply needed a house. Not a house *and* a second job. Then again, if working for Luke (in addition to *with* him) ended up as the only option...

No.

He clearly became uncomfortable with that once his aunt pounced her way into the conversation. Typical men. Afraid of overcommitting.

It was fine. She could have him as a daydream, instead. A handsome, if goofy, P.E. teacher who had no time for a relationship, probably, since he coached football and ran a bed-and-breakfast, too. Maybe they'd warm up to each other. Maybe they'd settle into something flirty. That might tide her over during the week. Then, she'd take to Louisville on the weekends. Reconnect with old friends. Drink wine and make eye contact with businessmen who were as busy as Luke but distant enough that Greta could write off their disinterest as a matter of fact. It was a sufferable rejection. Not an intimate one.

With Luke, she was too up close and personal. Too aware of how perfect he was. Talk about an enigma. Who the heck was he, anyway? This almost-local who juggled two jobs, ran his late grandmother's inn, and was clearly well loved by every single person who came into contact with him? If someone like that—someone who cut water boy deals with middle schoolers and volunteered at church... someone so *down to earth*—found cause to reject her, she wouldn't handle it well.

Businessmen or engineers or tech folks—they were way safer. They were naturally aloof, and their busy schedules had nothing to do with community outreach and everything to do with a facade. The same facade that had kept Greta from falling to pieces after her mother passed. A perfect, superficial life. No room for grit and truth and heart. No room for sweet nothings on the sofa with a pile of popcorn and a jug of sweet tea within reach. No room for the good stuff. Just the stuff that would carry Greta to and from a job that could fulfill her emotionally. A job that could save her from falling even further in love with

Maggie's family and the crazy mess of a big, happy family in her tiny, close-knit hometown.

***

Come ten-thirty, when they had their first break, Greta slipped her phone out of her purse. Sure enough, Rhett had sent a flurry of texts, confusing ramblings about the lack of rentals in town. His final message, and the most important one, was his conclusion that there were exactly three places in town with any ounce of potential, but it was looking like Greta might want to just stay in the barn. That, or else consider living in Louisville and commuting.

Commuting was out of the question. It would add extra time to her workday, and besides, if she was going to work in Hickory Grove then she would live there, too. It wasn't New York City. There was no subway. No fast-paced world in which to get lost. Just the good, hard work of a teacher.

Her eyes slid across the pictures Rhett had sent. Two of the three were definite negatives for her. Way out of her budget, made clear by the rent price indicated on their signage. She still had to get furniture (assuming the rentals were unfurnished), which meant the rent *had* to fit her budget.

The third photo, however, held some promise. It was a big house and a beautiful one. Probably too good to be true, in fact, since the sign did not indicate the cost of rent.

Two stories with peach paint and white trim, wildflowers. Landscaping spread from the mailbox on up to a beautiful little porch. It looked very familiar, though Greta couldn't pin it down. The sign in front simply read FOR RENT and listed two local numbers, both of which were neatly handwritten in thick black marker.

The teachers at her table had started complaining about some new policy regarding grades. Two wandered off for more coffee. Luke remained in his seat next to her, his leg bouncing up and down beneath the table. She kept herself from smiling and quickly tapped out a quick text to the first phone number. She left out any details and simply asked if it was still available. She didn't want to get her hopes up.

"Well, what do you think so far?"

Greta looked up, worried as though she'd been caught texting during class. It was Luke, testing the waters of conversation. This time, just between them.

She smiled at him. "It's... it's going well, I think. A lot like the other places I've been." She lifted her head to indicate the cafeteria and roaming faculty members.

He nodded. "So, you were saying before... about your family?" His face took on an almost pained expression, and Greta saw her opportunity to finish what she was saying, but her phone buzzed on her lap.

"I don't have a *family*, exactly. I mean, I *do* have a family. What I *meant* was..." A waiting text glowed from her lap, and she realized she couldn't properly explain herself while a possible landlord sat there, waiting for her reply. "Um, I'm so sorry. Mind if I just read my text?" She pointed to her device, and Luke nodded vigorously.

"Oh, yeah. Of course."

He took his phone out, too, mirroring her, as she read the reply to her inquiry.

I AM CURRENTLY DRIVING AND WILL ANSWER YOUR MESSAGE WHEN I ARRIVE AT MY DESTINATION. THIS IS AN AUTOMATED RESPONSE.

"Oh," Greta murmured.

Luke glanced at her. "Everything okay?"

She let out a small sigh. "Yes. I just... do you think I have time to make a quick phone call?" She scanned the podium for any action, but Mrs. Cook was nowhere to be seen.

He followed her gaze then nodded. "Yeah. I can come find you if they start before you're back."

Smiling, she thanked him and excused herself to the nearest bathroom, the girls' restroom. Same one from her days at H.G.M.S.

Once inside, Greta chuckled. It was just the same as she recalled. The dated stalls, etched in middle-school musings. The stall doors with embarrassingly wide gaps. The wall-length mirror where Greta and her friends would pat their hair down into place and apply no fewer than forty swipes of lip gloss.

Safely inside, she pulled Rhett's photo up again, briefly committing to her memory the second phone number. This time she would call. That way she didn't have to sneak a peek at her phone during the second session.

Just as she dialed, she heard shuffling come over the loudspeaker. Worried to miss anything, and aware that poor Luke wouldn't be able to retrieve her, Greta pressed the phone to her ear and stepped out of the bathroom.

It turned out that the distance from where she stood to the rest of the cafeteria was sufficiently private, and the noise she heard was the tech person, fiddling with the speakers. Mrs.

Cook could be spied whispering with the dean of students at his table.

Luke still sat where she'd left him, scrolling through his phone while the social studies teacher—Mark, was it?—gesticulated and chatted with the other English teachers.

The phone started to ring, and Greta turned away, focusing now on what she would say. She was from Hickory Grove, back in town with a full-time teaching position. She had enough for a deposit and would love to know if the place came furnished by any chance. Her expectations at bay, she held her breath.

A man's voice answered. Vaguely familiar, much like the house in her brother's photo. It was too garbled with background sounds for her to pin down.

"Hi," she answered. "I'm calling in regard to the house for rent on..." she realized she didn't have so much as a street address, "... the two-story house. I saw a sign for it with this phone number?" She squeezed her eyes shut and bit down on her bottom lip.

"Oh, of course. Yes. It's still available."

Now she *knew* she recognized the voice but still couldn't figure out whose it was.

"Terrific!" Greta answered, turning back around now that she had a little momentum. "Can you give me a little more information?"

"Sure, well it's a two-story like you mentioned. Three bedrooms, two baths. Great family home." The background noise made it hard to hear him again, and Greta began to wonder if it was the noise from her end or his. He went on with more details but kept cutting out.

She stopped him. "Sir? I'm so sorry, but it's a little hard to hear you. I'd hate to lose out on this, but is it alright if I call back during lunch or after work?" She winced, aware she might be cutting out on him, too.

"Actually, yes. I'll send you details via text, then you can call me back later. I'm free after three."

It was still hard to hear him well, but she put it all together and anxiously responded, "Perfect!"

They hung up, and she held her phone against her chest, praying the details he sent over would be something she could handle. A reasonable rate. A simple lease agreement. It would make everything perfect. She could return to her little hodge-podge table of English teachers and Luke and the Mark character and maybe, just maybe, focus on learning about her new school. And if she was *really* lucky, she could clear the vague misconception she floated out there that she *almost* had a family like some flakey floozy with a history of men or a long list of ones that got away or something. Or even a complicated family picture that was just too involved to discuss.

She wanted her colleagues to think of her just as she was: an efficient, capable, single woman on a mission to educate the children of Hickory Grove. No history of heartache. No drama. Just Greta.

As Greta neared her table, Luke was on his phone, texting frantically.

"I'm back," she chirped, setting her own device squarely on the table in front of her. Until Mrs. Cook resumed the meeting, she would be on the lookout. Then, like a good new hire, she'd tuck her phone away. In the meantime, she could hope and pray everything would work out.

"So," Luke said once he was done with his own business. "Have you found a place yet?"

Chapter 14—Luke

It was a risky move, to ask about the very thing that seemed to stand in their way of going from awkward strangers to comfortable colleagues.

Luke, however, was a risk-taker, by nature. Well, not *really*. But ever since Greta Houston took a step into his life, he felt like there was danger lurking around every corner. She was like a siren, and he had no interest in getting caught up in some unrequited crush with a big-city transplant. Even if she was originally a small-town girl, she still put on the act. Like she was there to work, and that was it. No more fish fries. Just teach and make subtle hints about a life she left behind. Luke looked to the future. He had a football program to run. P.E. students to blow a whistle at. No time for games.

Not only that, but now he was fielding phone calls about the Inn. Wasn't Liesel supposed to be on-call?

"Not yet, but I'm hopeful. Plus, it's not like I'm homeless." She laughed nervously, and Luke wanted to kick himself all over again.

"Oh, I didn't mean to imply..."

"No, no. It was just a joke." Her laughter fell away, and she glanced down at her phone.

Luke swallowed, his jaw tensing. Maybe she was texting with her boyfriend. Or husband, even. He wasn't totally certain there wasn't someone in the picture. After all, he couldn't count on any information that his aunt pieced together from her grapevine.

Once she set her phone back down, he got a text of his own to busy himself with. Usually, he'd have the darn thing stuffed away in his pocket. Luke wasn't the type to mindlessly scroll through silly videos or whatever, but it was pretty convenient that he was getting calls and texts about the Inn at the time that he needed to look a little less... *available.*

"Sorry. I need to answer this." He gestured down, and Greta smiled and nodded her permission, as though they were on a date or something. *In his dreams.*

As he read the message, pressure dissipated in Luke's head. Everything the inquiring woman wrote aligned with his search for a good tenant. He just needed to let her know of the terms of the lease. It had been a dealbreaker so far in wooing a prospective tenant-slash-manager—or *innkeeper*, as Liesel preferred to say.

He carefully considered his response. In the woman's message, she indicated the price was right but wanted to know more about the terms. Also, the address. This alarmed him. How did she see their sign if she didn't know where the house was?

Closing his eyes, he blew out a sigh. Probably a scam. He hated to call out an innocent person, but Luke wasn't going to pretend that her questions didn't add up. *Sorry, but don't you know where it is? You saw the sign, right?* He winced and wondered if he was being awkward or harsh, but one thing he knew was that if something smelled funny, then it probably was.

He hit send and squeezed his eyes shut.

"Everything okay?" Greta asked.

He peeked out at her from the corner of his eye then offered a tight, thin-lipped smile. "Yeah, just dealing with the

bed-and-breakfast. It's my second full-time job." It felt like a relief, confessing to her. Plus, she already knew about it, so maybe
she'd understand. "We're having a hard time finding a night
manager, as you can probably guess by now." As the words tum-
bled out of his mouth, he was reminded why Greta posed a
danger to him. Or, actually, why *Luke* posed a danger to *himself*
when he was talking to Greta.

It was the wrong thing to say, and he could see it in her eyes.
Maybe she felt slighted. Maybe she thought he was passively ag-
gressively reminding her about Fry-day and how she blew him
off when he and his aunt spelled out an opportunity for her to
move from Maggie's barn into her own place.

"Sure, sure," she replied, then took a sip from her water
bottle as her eyes slid past him and around the room. "I was
almost a landlord back in Indianapolis," she began, her voice
low. Their eyes locked, and he knew the *almost family* story
was there, somewhere. He could see she wanted to share it, but
feedback screeched across the cafeteria. Greta and others threw
their hands to their ears.

Mrs. Cook stood at the podium and held the microphone
out away from herself, dragging everyone off their extended
break with an apology. "Sorry! Technical difficulties," she joked
as the projector in the back finally buzzed to life, and a Power-
Point illuminated the drop-down screen. "Next, I'd like to go
over some of the data and survey results I mentioned earlier.
Barb will bring around paper and markers." She then went on
to explain that they weren't only going to *look* at data. They
were going to *dig into it!*

A quiet moan rippled across the cafeteria, but Mrs. Cook,
in her position behind the podium, was immune, pushing

ahead with enthusiasm for getting to *practice what we preach* and *turn the content into a student-led learning activity!*

"I sort of hate this stuff," he whispered to his table, glancing at Greta to see if he could bring her back around. The others agreed in hushed giggles, and Mark let out a long sigh, launching into a tirade against buzzwords and busy work.

Greta, however, was frowning down at the phone in her lap, her focus elsewhere again.

A chill climbed up his spine. Was she dealing with the family stuff? Did it have to do with her *almost rental property*? Or her current living situation thing, again? He didn't dare ask. It was *not* his business.

Discreetly checking his own phone for a reply from the interested tenant, he started to feel hot. Suffocated, even. He pinched the fabric of his polo and tugged it quickly a few times then put his phone to sleep, determined to set the issue aside and focus on school for the day. Liesel said she'd handle it. So, if the person *did* need to talk urgently, well, they'd have to wait for him to get out of work or call Liesel again. Maybe he ought to text that exact message, in fact. Especially if there was some confusion over where the house was. The house that this person obviously *saw* already.

Pushing air through his teeth, he dragged his phone back out to send the follow-up text. The recipient, whose name he didn't know, had not yet replied. He began to write that she would have to call the other number on the sign. *You know*, he typed, *the sign at the house you looked at?*

Out of the corner of his eye, he noticed Greta, furiously tapping away on her own device. He couldn't make out her message or the contact she was writing to, but something felt, well, *funny*.

That's when it clicked.

His chest tightened. He swallowed and looked again at Greta. A thrill zipped through him.

He hesitated only momentarily before picking his phone back up and deleting his draft. He started again, as she sat next to him, clearly struggling with what *he* had written.

Can we talk in person?

Glancing up to ensure the others were sufficiently absorbed in Mark's tale about the glory days of teaching when you got a roster and a blackboard and lecture for an hour straight, Luke bit down on his lip and hit send. Adjacent to him, Susan dragged a marker across the paper, dutifully following Mrs. Cook's directions on how to shape their graphic organizer and begin analyzing the data. Next to him, Greta paused in her frantic texting and tucked her phone between her legs then looked up, her features softer, now.

"What do you think, Miss Houston?" Luke asked, amusement glinting in his eyes. Her face reddened, and he felt a little guilty. Still, he couldn't resist. "The data Mrs. Cook is projecting. About phones in the classroom. Should we limit our technology in our lessons or expand on it?"

Mark's voice faded away. The others waited, Susan with her marker ready to document whatever brilliant thing the new teacher had to share.

Greta pushed her hair out of her face and smiled at him. "Technology is important," she started, the others rapt. "Especially in a rural community. We should provide opportunities for it. Not shy away."

"But don't you think..." Luke went on, propping his elbows on the table, his own secret acting as ammunition. Suddenly, the beautiful new hire was no longer bringing him to his knees. Suddenly, he had the upper hand. And though Luke knew that teasing her like this could totally backfire, he figured he had nothing to lose.

After all, the person texting him wasn't *really* interested in renting his mamaw's house.

The person texting him didn't know it was Mamaw's house at all. She didn't know that she stumbled across The Hickory Grove Inn, and that it wasn't just a house for rent. It was the *Innkeeper's House*.

"Don't I think what?" Greta replied, a little edge to her voice that time.

The person texting him didn't know she was texting him at all.

Luke met her gaze, pausing only briefly. "Don't you think we should put the phones away and talk *in person*?"

Chapter 15—Greta

If swooning were an option, she'd have swooned. Right then and there.

Greta's head swelled to the point of near bursting. "Yes," she murmured, blinking slowly. The conversation among the others drifted away, half the table arguing in favor of cell phones in the class, half opposed.

Meanwhile, Luke kept his eyes on her. Subtlety was nearly impossible, and Greta couldn't bear to have her face flush again. Not on her first day. Not in front of him.

"It's you?" she whispered, glancing at him from beneath her eyelashes.

His reply came low, even. "I thought you weren't interested?"

"I never said that."

Luke lifted a skeptical eyebrow. "You never *said* you were interested."

Mrs. Cook strolled by, treating them like a group of students, inspecting and praising their four-square about the parent concern of Phones in the Classroom. Satisfied, she floated off. The rest of the table broke away into gossip and banter, leaving Greta and Luke to resume their conversation more comfortably. With less whispers. Less secrecy.

Though, Greta quite liked the secret conversation.

A chill danced up her spine, and goosebumps tingled across her limbs.

Not once in her years as a teacher or sub had she ever engaged in a flagrant flirtation at work.

"Are we talking about the same thing?" Greta couldn't help it. Her cheeks burned. The skin on her arms turned cold and splotchy as if every bit of blood in her body had rushed to her head to help keep her brain functioning.

Luke cracked a grin. "Yes?"

She laughed, which helped to clear her head somewhat. "Maggie told me that your rental house comes with a stipulation."

"And what's that?" he replied.

"Whoever rents it must also take care of the bed-and-breakfast."

His smile dissipated. "Well," he began, "not *exactly*, but yes."

She frowned.

Luke blew out a sigh and pushed his fingers through his hair. "We need someone on call at night. Someone on the property. We don't keep the desk open past eight. So, it's sort of like a twelve-hour shift, but you can go to sleep or whatever. Just keep your phone on. My aunt and I will handle the situation, but since we don't have a night clerk, it's nice to have an available staff member." He shook his head. "It sounds weird, I know. Liesel would do it if she could stand to be in there, but she can't. Not now. I've been staying over as much as possible, but with football season, it's going to be hard. That's why the rent is crazy low. Plus, if whoever moves in wants to take on more, we'll cut the rent further."

Greta mulled it over. It wasn't as bad as she previously thought. Maggie mischaracterized the whole thing. Still, was it a *good* idea to complicate her life even further? First, she stole the barn from Gretchen. Now, she was going to take up in the

Hart family heirloom? The worst thing she could do was become entangled in local drama.

What if there was more to it than just being "on call" overnight? What if she developed feelings for Luke then he broke her heart? What if she found a better job somewhere else the following summer?

"What are the other terms?" she asked.

He paused, glancing around the table then dipping his chin. "My aunt has a rental agreement typed up. I just need to run to my classroom to print it out. If you'd like, I could give it to you to look at during lunch?"

She swallowed. It already felt like a big commitment just to look at the agreement, even if she wasn't signing it. What if she couldn't handle taking phone calls over night? What if a real emergency *did* happen?

"What kind of emergencies?" she asked, her eyebrows furrowed deep.

Luke chuckled. "Nothing, really. We're hardly ever booked up, and people who stay there are often regulars. The ones who aren't regulars, well, I give them my phone number. Mainly, we hope to cover household expenses like utilities. If I'm being honest with you, Greta," he lowered his gaze, and she thought she saw a little color climb up his neck. "We just want someone to take care of Mamaw's house. At least for a little while. Until we can get back on track." He glanced up at her, an earnestness in his eyes.

"It could work," she started to answer, chewing on her lower lip. "The price is right. It's just... would it be, like a..." Words escaped her. Mrs. Cook had returned to the podium and was about to send them into another activity, no doubt.

"Conflict of interest," Luke answered, his tone turning cold. He shook his head. "I understand. You don't know me. I, well *I* don't know you. Yeah, it's weird. You've got enough on your plate without having to deal with living in your co-worker's dead grandmother's house." Mirthlessness filled his face, and Greta tried to decide if he was being sincere or not. He made good points, but then, whenever did a landlord know his tenant before they signed a contract?

"Can I see it?" she said at last, hope clinging to each word.

Luke's eyes flashed. "Of course you can. Yes, of course. We can go there right after work."

"It's a date," she said, out of sheer habit. Wincing at herself as Luke chuckled, Greta shook her head. "Yes, I mean. That's perfect."

The rest of the day dragged on. At lunch, instead of going with Luke to print a copy of the lease agreement, Greta begged off to track down the secretary, Barb. Mrs. Cook had indicated that Barb would deliver her teaching contract before the end of the day and *not to worry! You'll be paid for showing up for pre-service training!*

When she found the woman, Barb was juggling a tower of freshly printed packets.

"Let me help you," Greta offered, taking half the stack and inhaling the sterile scent of hot paper and ink.

The woman was grateful, and Greta was happy to get to know her a little better.

"How's your first day going?" Barb asked as she took short, choppy steps from the doorway of the cafeteria over to her table.

"It's going well. Do you need help handing this out, or...?"

"No, no. I'll handle, darlin'. Go get you something to eat before those men make their way down the line." She nodded toward the buffet tables and laughed to herself.

"Actually, Miss Barb," Greta went on, stalling nervously, "Mrs. Cook said I could see you about getting my contract?" She hated that it came out like a question, but, well, it was awkward to have to prompt her employers. At previous districts, the contract was available well before Greta began working. There she was, half a day in and not yet on the payroll. She licked her lips.

"Oh, right. Yes, well, I haven't gotten it down from the district office yet. Why don't we check together right after the in-service today? Will that be all right?"

Greta flashed a smile. "Sure!"

***

The afternoon training meant a brief goodbye from Luke, which was okay. She could use the distance to really think about the rental and if she really wanted to make a go of entering into an agreement with someone she was... well, *attracted* to.

English department meetings, grade level meetings, and then classroom work time whirred by. Come quarter to three, Greta was exhausted. Mainly, she'd thumbed her way through the book closet that spread between her room and the other English teacher's. Ideas for unit plans and lessons took shape in her imagination. She jotted notes onto a whiteboard that sat propped up against the doorway. Shakespeare was questionable at that age, but they did have copies of *Twelfth Night*, which might work. More interesting than that were volumes of Poe and an Agatha Christie title. The hint of excitement was starting to creep in where dread formerly lived, fluttering like butterflies in her stomach and her heart. Maybe Middle School wouldn't be too bad, after all.

Still, unease persisted not in Greta's heart but in her head. If there was one thing she'd taken from her time in Indianapolis... her time with *Kadan*, it was that words (and even fine diamonds) were never enough. *Promises* were not enough. *Deals*... not enough.

Closing the door to the book closet, Greta took up her satchel and the tote in which she had neatly stowed her New Teacher Packet and every single handout from the day. Then, she left to find Miss Barb.

"I was just coming by to scoop you on up and sweep you upstairs, dear heart." The portly, kind secretary waddled down the hall toward Greta, who smiled with relief.

The district office hung squarely on the second floor of Hickory Grove Middle School's building, convenient and intimidating, to be sure.

Greta remembered as a child once glimpsing the superintendent escaping from the second floor down to the parking lot, like Bigfoot or some legend. She shuddered even now at the thought. They climbed the stairs together, side by side, Miss Barb pausing every few steps to catch her breath.

Once they made it upstairs, Greta inspected the hallowed space. Blown-up photographs of Hickory Grove students from yesteryear glimmered from behind their frames, staring from the past at Greta, pulling her back to ancient history. A time when her mother was alive. A student there, probably.

An invisible magnetic force pulled her toward the images.

"Hello-ooo!" Barb yodeled at the barren front desk.

Greta turned around and followed the woman's searching gaze down a seemingly empty corridor.

"Hmm." Barb tapped a long, painted fingernail on the wooden desk. She appeared to be considering whether to breach the invisible barrier between her station as a school secretary and the world of district leadership. "They don't usually leave until five," she went on, offering a sympathetic smile. "Probably in a meeting, dear."

Greta checked her wristwatch. She had promised to follow Luke to The Hickory Grove Inn at three sharp. She had his number. She could cancel. But should she?

Or should she trust that a contract was drawn up, ready for her signature, waiting on someone's desk just yards away?

"That's all right, Miss Barb." Greta shrugged happily. "I'm sure I can get it tomorrow. I'm not going anywhere."

But as she said it, her stomach churned. Her mind flitted back to Kadan again. The broken promises of principals who'd assured her that her sub gig would turn into a full-time classroom position. Then again, she hadn't exactly heard from any other school anywhere she had applied.

Plus, she had a *date* now. A date with a bed-and-breakfast and the house next door and the man who owned it. The man who needed her help.

Chapter 16—Luke

Luke had exactly one hour before practice. One hour to woo Greta. Not necessarily into taking on the house, either. Sitting next to her all morning had rattled his brain and stirred his heart to life. Gone was the fleeting temptation to bounce out of Hickory Grove. Gone was the fear about what would become of the bed-and-breakfast. In fact, he wasn't too concerned what would become of it at all. He'd figure it out. He would. Even football felt a little less important.

All Luke could think about now was being close to Greta again, even if just for an hour.

She appeared from the side door. Her large, preppy leather satchel overpowering her frame, Greta strode taller in matching leather sandals—were they high heels? He didn't know the slightest thing about women's fashion. He'd never taken notice! Now, everything about her mattered, even her shoes. If Luke didn't know any better, he'd say he was falling for the girl.

Unfortunately, he was at risk for complicating matters. Serious risk. Maybe, though, that didn't matter. So long as Greta found a safe place in town where she could hang her satchel and slip out of her leather high-heeled sandal shoes. A place for her to take care of... that would make him happy. Even if their growing flirtation went nowhere, it could be a good idea. It could be good for *her*, even. Especially, if the rumor was true.

If she was mending a broken heart. Something he knew little about but which he wasn't afraid of. At least, he wasn't afraid of *other* people's broken hearts.

"Hi." He smiled at her, blood pounding in his ears.

She grinned back, but something felt off. Was she disappointed? If so, about what? He was in no position to nag her about the intricacies of her emotions and expressions and her leather satchel and her leather shoes and whether they were high heels or sandals or whatever the heck.

"Hi." Greta raised a tote bag in her other hand, gesturing indirectly toward her little silver car. "I'm just over there." He wondered if he should volunteer to give her a ride instead of her following him, but then she added, "I know where it is, so don't worry about losing me."

Luke chuckled. "You think I could lose you in Hickory Grove traffic?"

Greta shrugged. "Since I was here last, I can see a notable change in the population." She lifted an eyebrow at him then expertly slid a pair of jet-black sunglasses from her tote and pushed them up her nose. A shadow fell over her face, hiding her faint freckles and playing foil to her bright blonde hair. She was like a California transplant, more foreign than him, somehow. Like someone who left so long ago that coming back could only ever be a vacation.

He mirrored her eyebrow wiggle, his lips curling into a smile. "Has your hometown changed that much?"

Her smile slipped from her face, but he couldn't tell what was going on in her eyes. "Yes and no." She pulled the glasses off and used them to point south. "You know, the place where I grew up is that way."

He turned to follow her gesture. "What happened to it?"

"The house?" She continued to stare off.

"Yes."

A sigh lifted her chest, and for the first time, Luke saw more than a bubbly personality and positive spirit. He saw something else entirely. Something deeper. She smiled at him. "My parents sold it when I left for college. They left, too. Moved out east, where my mom was from. She was never as tied to this place as my dad was. Even though she came here for high school, it was just..." Greta frowned.

"Just what?"

"Just where they met. And, I guess, where they raised us."

Luke knew a little about Greta's mother. Liesel filled in a few blanks for him. Tidbits she'd culled from the Ladies Auxiliary or knew herself.

"What do you mean 'just met?' 'Just raised you?'" He wasn't sure why, but he needed her to love Hickory Grove. He needed her to see it for more than *just* whatever.

"I guess I see people like Maggie and her family and even my brother Rhett, and they are so *tied* to this place. Like it's *more* than a place to live." She flashed a smile at him and put her sunglasses back on. "My mom wasn't very sentimental. It made things easier, in some ways. Nothing to get too attached to." Greta spoke in a way that indicated that *she* knew that *he* knew about her mother. Maybe that was the small town in her. The assumption that her business wasn't her own. He wasn't sure what to say. It didn't matter. Greta continued for the both of them. "When she was sick, we had to sell some land down past the old schoolhouse. My dad's family's property. Rhett tried to get it back, but I guess someone bought it and started building on it. I'm not sure who. I wish I knew. I'd give him a piece of my mind. You don't do that to your community. To your friends, you know? You make it so they can keep what's theirs." She let out a sigh. "I don't know why I'm unloading all this on you. I guess you probably want to get going."

Luke swallowed. He wasn't the crying type, but Greta, there in the middle of the H.G.M.S. parking lot in broad daylight, was about to coax tears from him. All he could do was shake his head. If he said anything, the floodgates would unleash. He'd humiliate himself. He'd spill his guts about how much he *loved* feeling at home in Hickory Grove. That *of course* it was more than *just a place to live*. Maybe they were more different than he'd figured.

"Anyway," she shook her head, her smile hanging across her mouth, wobbly like she too felt the pull of emotion, "I just meant that I can understand why you're trying to hang on to the bed-and-breakfast and your mamaw's house. I would do the same thing."

He smiled back and choked down his feelings. He could hug her. Maybe he should hug her? No. Not yet. "I appreciate that. Maybe one day Liesel or I will live there. I could see that happening. For now, though, we just need an innkeeper. Someone to keep the sofa warm and the fridge full of sweet tea. You know?"

"I sure do." She sniffled and drew the back of her hand across her forehead. "Well, then. Should we go?"

"Yep." Before jumping into his truck, he winked at Greta. "In case you *do* get lost, it's a left then your second right after the stop sign. A stone's throw up the old dirt road, and you've made it to Hickory Grove's premier bed-and-breakfast."

"Hickory Grove's *only* bed-and-breakfast," she called over her shoulder.

"Depends on your definition!" he hollered back, chuckling again to himself. After all, in their little corner of Kentuckiana, southern hospitality ran rampant. Anyone with a bed could offer breakfast, too.

Luke just hoped that Greta was looking for something more than that.

Chapter 17—Greta

"Wow," she breathed as they stepped inside of the Inn. Luke wanted to start there, so she could see what she might be getting herself into.

In all her years growing up in Hickory Grove, Greta had never once stepped a foot inside the place. It was a weird thing to think about now. Logical, sure. But still bizarre to know absolutely nothing about one of your town's fixtures.

One time, when Greta was in elementary school, her parents had a bad fight. Her mother left the house, and—being that cell phones didn't exist yet, at least not in Hickory Grove—Greta and Rhett didn't know where she'd left to. Her family was out in Philly. Greta had initially suspected the poor woman, angry and wayward, had retreated there, to the little Inn at the top of Overlook Lane. When her mother returned just hours later, it was clear by the blanket of silt on her station wagon that she'd just driven around the area, rolling between green hills, kicking up pebbles and dust and cursing out their dad in privacy.

The whole ordeal had struck Greta as traumatizing and dramatic. In her mind, The Hickory Grove Inn was this scary, towering place that offered refuge to peeved-off mothers who needed to get away from their families.

But then, Greta's mother wasn't actually like that. Probably, she was just a little burnt out. Raising kids and stuck at home all the time had made her a little batty. That, plus, she'd always been more interested in anywhere other than Hickory Grove. Greta never knew why. Until she got sick. That's when the advice and pearls of wisdom flooded out. The woman had used her remaining days to teach Greta everything she could think of about life, but none of it stuck save for one reminder: *Find what makes you happy, and do it, Greta.*

The implication was painfully obvious. Whatever would have made her mother happy, well, she never got to do it. Was it the right job? Was it more children? Less? A different town? She hadn't said, which only left Greta to search and search and search until the search turned into a hunt for some truth about who she was and what made her, *Greta*, happy.

Forever, Greta figured that teaching was that thing. After all, for most of her adulthood she was only marginally happy, and certainly never satisfied. Then she started dating. Fervently searching for someone—*anyone*—good enough to pull off a shotgun wedding. The hunt became especially desperate once her mother fell sick. If Greta found someone passable and married him, then maybe her mother would die happy. Maybe her mother could see that Greta had found happiness, too. *Nothing to worry about, Mom! I've got a rich husband and a great condo! We're going to build a perfect house and have two perfect kids, just like you did! We'll be so* happy.

"Greta, meet Stella, our day clerk."

Luke's voice snapped her out of the reverie. She pushed a finger to the corner of her eye and smiled at the woman who appeared from the eating area off to the right.

"Hi, great to meet you." Greta stuck out her hand, and Stella shook it before rambling on various details about her personal life and notes about the Inn.

Greta listened politely, but her mind wandered. It struck her that the place was nothing like the vision she'd conjured in her mind's eye. Dated, yes. Towering and imposing, hardly. And certainly not a place to escape from reality, if that's what young Greta ever thought her mother was doing.

Frankly, it was no wonder the Inn barely squeaked by (*if* that was true; Gretchen claimed she'd overheard Liesel bemoaning the financial situation at Mally's one day). The outside was charming and quaint enough to draw curiosity. But the inside swept you back in time. It looked like Maggie's farmhouse probably did before she started renovating. Lots of wood. Little else. Where were the lace doilies and homey touches?

Once they made their way over to the house behind the Inn, Mamaw Hart's old house, she found them. The lace doilies and homey touches. The poor old woman probably snuck out every last blanket and tablecloth and linen and found a place for each one in her home.

"You and Liesel... you left all of this? For... for a tenant to use?" Greta didn't mean to pass judgment, but she was confused. Sure, she was glad to see the place fully furnished on the one hand. On the other, she was alarmed that Liesel and Luke had left so much of June Hart's possessions behind, to be used by some... *stranger*.

Luke shook his head. "Liesel's basement and mine are filled to the brim with Mamaw's things. And we have a storage unit, too."

Greta frowned. Delicately, she asked, "Was she a... a... a hoarder?"

"It wasn't like that," he replied. "I mean, looking at it now, all you see are her personal effects. But all of this is just the bare minimum of what Mamaw collected and carefully organized. She had afghans folded and shelved in one closet. Drapes and linens in another. Lots of clothes. Lots of them. Liesel couldn't stand to go through her hope chest, but that's in her basement, waiting to be unpacked, still. We just left what we thought would look nice in here. I guess it's sort of a living memorial." He glanced away and fiddled with a crystal bowl that sat on the table by the front door. "Anyway, feel free to look around. Take your time."

She nodded and started through the place. It wasn't as cluttered as she initially thought. The living room, or parlor as it might have been years back, was small; an old tube TV complete with rabbit ears sat on a short table across from a red velvet sofa. Across the back of a sofa draped a yellow afghan and between the sofa and television set sprawled an oval black-and-red braided rug. But no doodads or knickknacks cluttered the space.

Beyond the parlor, more braided rugs carried her across sturdy hardwood floors and into the kitchen, which took her further back in time. A farmhouse sink, white porcelain, acted like the centerpiece along a Formica counter. The butcher block island crowded the space, but the only appliances in sight were an old Frigidaire, a rusty little toaster, and a potbellied stove.

"When was this place built?" Greta wondered aloud.

"My great grandfolks built it around the turn of the century, I think." Luke ran his hand along the round wooden kitchen table. "This was all here when I was a kid. This is where Mamaw put out the food for Christmas or Easter brunch. We ate wherever we could find a seat."

"Is it hard to let someone else move in?" she asked, fearful she might come across as prying.

Luke's eyes flashed, and his Adam's apple bobbed up and down. "Yes," he said, sniffing. "Especially for my aunt."

Greta studied him for a beat after he looked away. His good looks and fit build belied a tenderness. The P.E. teachers and football coaches Greta had known in her life came across as spud-chewing, leather-necked good-old-boys with one thing on their minds: winning a game.

Luke was softer. Quieter. More anxious, though still assured. Deep in thought. Kind.

"How is your season shaping up?" the question fell out of her mouth, in it an accusation, as if she wanted to test him. See if his gentle way was effective in his career of choice.

He raised his eyebrows. "Oh, um. Good. We're looking good." He shoved his hands into his pockets. "Do you want to see upstairs?"

She nodded, and they climbed the narrow wooden case together, Greta behind. She forced herself to keep a little distance. Being too close to Luke might just suffocate her. Once he reached the landing, he offered his hand. It was an unnecessary gesture. There was no danger, but still she took it, her breath growing shallow.

Upstairs, the three bedrooms were small but neatly appointed. Two of them offered double beds. Heavy quilts spread across the foot of each. In the third bedroom, an antique roll top desk ran the length of a windowless wall.

"We decided to leave it. It was my grandad's," Luke said from behind her. She nodded then turned. "I love it here. I can't believe you haven't found someone... or that Liesel or you haven't moved in yourselves."

"We have our own houses," Luke answered. "I like being close to the school. Liesel is near Little Flock. But maybe one day we will. When it gets easier."

She nodded. She understood. After all, wasn't it Greta who agreed to sell off the Houston family acreage? She could have found money elsewhere. But she went to the land, first. As if to shake herself free of that attachment. Rid her life of the history of Hickory Grove. It made far less sense that Greta was so keen to move on. She had a happy upbringing. No tragedy existed for either her or her brother in that town. And still, she suggested they dump what they had. Guilt crawled along beneath her skin. She slid a finger along her hairline and fanned her face.

"We have window AC units," Luke said, pointing behind her to a little white box that sat on the corner of the floor. "Sorry about the heat."

"Oh, it's no problem."

Smiling, Luke waved behind them toward the open door. "There's not much else to see, but it's pretty simple. One year. Or month-to-month. Whatever works for you. The rate is pretty set, but I might be able to get some wiggle room from Liesel if you need."

"No, no. The price is great. The terms are great. I think I could do the on-call thing at night, too."

"That's mostly just for peace of mind, you know. It's really not a big deal. We give the guests Liesel's number and mine, too. Just so you know."

Greta's brows furrowed over her head. There was no real catch. Just a family of mourners trying to make ends meet while they preserved a piece of their past.

"I love it, actually. Really, I do, Luke." Was that the first time she'd called him by name? The first time she'd said *Luke*, the syllables lolling from her tongue in lazy, sweet sounds. Their eyes met. She looked away. "Coach," she corrected herself, a small smiling curving her mouth up.

"Call me Luke," he replied, his voice low. "I'm glad you love it. I do, too." Tension buzzed between them. Over the house or their words or the school year ahead or whatever was going on... she felt it like pulsing electricity.

She inhaled sharply. "I haven't gotten my contract from school yet." Her smile slipped away, and worry took shape on her face. "Is that the norm?"

He licked his lips and his eyebrows raised. "Oh? Oh, well. I'm not sure. I mean, I got mine at the end of last year." He laughed nervously. "I'm sure you'll get it soon. Did you talk to Miss Barb?"

She nodded. "And we went upstairs to the D.O. No one was around, though."

He shrugged. "Hickory Grove is a slow place. But don't worry," he rushed to add, "I'm sure it's just sitting on someone's desk waiting for your signature." Again, a nervous chuckle followed.

"Yeah," Greta replied. Though she didn't know Luke, and she didn't even know Miss Barb or Mrs. Cook or anyone else at the school *she* had attended years before, she could choose to trust them, as uneasy as it made her. That quiet voice inside called to her again. *A bird in the hand.* So, too, did Greta hear her mother's words. *Find what makes you happy.* Contract or not, it occurred to Greta she'd never been quite so happy. She and Rhett were closer than ever, even if he was so aloof or dense that he sent her the photo of The Hickory Grove Inn, knowing full well that Maggie and Greta already agreed it was a bad idea for her.

Then again, was her brother being aloof?

Or was he being... intentional?

Regardless, their new bond was the only thing to reinvigorate Greta's spirits. Her newfound friendship with Maggie and forging a mentorship with sweet Gretchen. Little Briar, and Ky and Dakota. The farm and the barn and the fresh air and country backroads... all of it made her happy. Unquantifiably so, even.

And then there was Luke, this newcomer in her life. Someone with ties to the town but with the Louisville upbringing. The worldliness a person could possess just by virtue of the fact that they were born in a high-rise hospital rather than by the local midwife. Greta had often longed for that worldliness—to feel inside of her what it was like to live near a mall or cross the street at a stoplight with rush hour traffic whirring parallel to her. It was almost like that in Luke, God was bringing the big city to the country, as if that was even possible.

Greta hoped it was. Maybe then, she could stop searching.

Now, they stood together at the base of the staircase, Luke at the very bottom, Greta on the first step, her face level with his. The door stood closed just feet away, shutting the world out and keeping them in this tenuous privacy. From beneath her eyelashes, she looked up at Luke. He cleared his throat. Greta bit down on her bottom lip.

Swallowing, she swayed forward. What was she going to do? Tell him she wanted to rent his house? Grab the back of his neck and pull him into a kiss like some sort of tragic heroine in a black-and-white film?

He put his hand on the bannister, pulling himself closer to her, too, and ridiculously, thoughts of Kadan stirred to life in her brain. She tried to push them out, but dizziness took over anyway, blurring her vision momentarily.

"Are you okay?" Luke asked.

Her phone buzzed in her hand. She blinked. "Oh. Yes." It came out on a whisper, and she glanced at the screen, trying to hide how deeply she was blushing. "I have to take this." It was a fib. She didn't recognize the number. Could be spam for all she knew.

"Go ahead." Luke tucked his hands back into his pockets and strode to the door, opening it and stepping outside without closing it behind him.

She tapped *Accept*. "Hello?" Irritation swelled in her voice. She had a chance, and she blew it. A chance to say yes. And she blew it.

"Hi, is this Greta Houston?"

A flat voice came across the line, but Greta sensed it was no spam caller.

"Yes, this is she."

"Hi, Greta, this is Dawn Roberts with Chicago Public Schools."

Chapter 18—Luke

Once he was outside, Luke's heartbeat returned to normal, beating steadily in his chest, satisfied that everything went well.

Better than well.

Luke had dang near kissed the girl. He nearly peeled back the layer of decency, lifted her chin to his face, and kissed her. And he didn't even know her!

Now, he was going to be late for practice. While tapping out a quick text to Mark that he'd be on his way in a few, a new text came in from Liesel.

Well?

He glanced toward the door, but Greta's back was turned, her hand on the bannister where his had been moments before. His breath hitched as he replied to his aunt.

Went well but no confirmation yet. I think she wants it.

Greta seemed interested. Very interested. But maybe her interest was in something else. He couldn't tell. But interest was good. It was good. He ran a hand across his mouth and glanced at Liesel's quick response.

Can you lock her in right now?

His aunt's urgency caught him off guard. As he was about to reply, Greta appeared at the top of the porch steps.

Her face was darker, more serious. "Something's come up."

"Oh. Okay," Luke replied, confused. "Is everything all right?"

"That was weird." As she said it, she trotted down the steps and held her hand out, her phone face up. "I just got a call." A pleading look took over her face as she stated the obvious, but his bewilderment only deepened.

"Are you okay, Greta?"

With her phone still poised expectantly in her hand, she licked her lips, the dark expression turning to something akin to surprise. Not quite shock. But surprise. "I just got a call from Chicago Public Schools."

"Okay?"

Was that where she worked before? Did something go wrong with her references? Was that why she hadn't gotten a contract?

"I applied there last week," Greta explained.

The words knocked the wind out of him. "But you're here now." It was all he could muster.

"I know," she answered. Thoughtfulness replaced her surprise and softened her face, as though this were a *decision* she was going to have to make.

He simply shrugged and repeated himself. "You're here now. Right?" She'd been at the in-service with him all day. She worked in her classroom, like every other teacher at H.G.M.S.

"Right," Greta replied. Then she shook her head and smiled. "Right. I'm here now."

Fresh air filled his lungs, and he smiled again. "Welp," he went on, stalling for something else to add.

"Yeah," she agreed halfheartedly. There was no affirmation in the word. Only doubt.

"What about the house?" He waved his hand up at the place, its peach paint taking on shadows as the sun angled behind it. He glanced at his phone. Mark hadn't answered. His draft to Liesel sat waiting. The excitement and buzz that had coursed through him petered out now. In its place, lukewarm disappointment.

Greta nodded, frowning. "It's perfect, really. I'm surprised by how perfect it is." Then, as though she was brainstorming privately, she went on, her eyes darting around. "It's just a year. You all might want it back after a year anyway. That would give me time to figure things out. I could save up for something else, what with the low rate. A down payment. Gretchen gets the barn back. It's not far from school, of course. And Rhett is nearby. And..." She squinted up at him, light glinting in her eyes.

He smiled. "And... you've got a great landlord. Is that what you were going to say?"

She smiled back. "Actually, that might be the biggest reason to say yes."

The rollercoaster launched him again into a thrill ride of emotion. His pulse quickened. Should he make a move? Or should he pin her down on the lease? Luke pushed his hand through his hair and forced himself to play it cool. "Should I have my aunt bring over the paperwork?"

But her answer came like a kick to the face.

"Can I think about it?"

***

"What's there to think about?" Liesel asked over the phone as Luke drove to the football field. Disappointment didn't begin to describe how he felt.

"Maybe she doesn't want to deal with the Inn, too."

Liesel scoffed. "There's nothing to deal with. She gets a great house for a low price. Listen, Luke. I talked to Gary."

His blood turned to ice in his veins.

"Aunt Liesel," he answered his voice cold.

"Now, just listen, Luke. I want Greta in there as much or more than you. She's a doll. Fern thinks you two would make a great couple, too."

He winced and shook his head.

Liesel went on. "But a bird in the hand, Luke. A bird in the hand. Our priority is paying the bills."

"Oh, come on. You're afraid, Liesel."

It was the first time in his life he didn't address her by Aunt. It was an overstep. A dangerous one. More disrespectful than calling her out for her obvious fear.

"Excuse me?" Each word cut across the line like a dagger.

"You're afraid. You're too afraid to hold on to the past to preserve it. You don't want to see it. You can't face it. You can't handle that she died, but you have to. You know as well as I do that we can float the Inn. We can float the house, if need be, too. You're letting fear drive you. *Gary Hart*, of all people? Did you know he bought the Houston land some years ago?"

"What are you talking about, Luke?"

"Never mind that." He shook his head and put his truck in park, facing the football field. Lines of athletes darted along the grass in conditioning drills. Mark stood next to the goal post. Assistants spanned out around the field, their clipboards poised. None of it mattered. Not football. Not even beautiful Greta. Not if his aunt was going to throw away the one thing he'd come to accept as his in the world.

His father's childhood home. His grandmother's only house. The business his grandparents had carried on in sturdy old Hart tradition. He might have been moved to sell before. But not now. Not after walking the place with Greta, exploring his own personal history through her awestruck reaction to it all. Even if she didn't say yes, he could see what the place meant. The potential it had. It just needed TLC. A special touch.

And if Liesel were unwilling to take it on, then he would. With or without his hot-and-cold new co-worker.

"I'll buy you out," he said at last.

The line went deadly quiet.

Luke repeated himself. "I said I'll buy you out."

"I heard you," she answered.

"Well?"

He shifted under his seatbelt, pulling the strap tighter even though he was about to get out of the truck.

"Luke, I don't *want* to sell to Gary. And I'm not afraid. I just don't think we can manage it. I'm being practical. And what does the Houston family land have to do with any of this?"

"Nothing," he muttered, his pulse slowing. He wanted to scream. Why couldn't Greta commit? Why couldn't Liesel commit? Why was *Luke*, this thirty-something football coach, more interested in a small-town bed-and-breakfast than the two women in his life?

Was Greta *in* his life? He wondered about that and pounded a fist on the steering wheel. No. She made it clear she wasn't. And besides, they'd only ever met three times. Who was he kidding? She was more interested in Chicago, apparently.

"I'll buy you out," he whispered again.

"I don't know what to do, Luke," Liesel replied, her voice as low as his.

"You're not going to sell Mamaw's house. Or the Inn. Especially not to *Gary*. He already owns half the town. Mamaw wasn't his grandmother. And if you're really set on renting, which I get, I do; well, I don't know about Greta, but we can figure it out. Okay?"

The sound of whistles bounced off the field and trilled in through his cracked window.

"I gotta go, Aunt Liesel. Practice."

"Luke," she said, her voice softer now. "Let me talk to the girls. Maybe we can bring her around."

"What do you mean?"

"I'm getting my hair done today. At Maggie's. Let me see what I can find out. Okay?"

He thanked her and hung up. But a sinking feeling overcame him. Maybe a charming little grandmother house wasn't what Greta wanted in life. Images of her black sunglasses and fancy shoes and bag cut across his mind. Maybe what Greta wanted was to be far away from her little hometown. Maybe, if the D.O. dropped the ball on her contract, that's where she would wind up.

And all he would be left with was a charming little grandmother house and a dated bed-and-breakfast.

Even worse? The one girl who had caught his eye in ages could slip through his fingers.

He jogged up to the field, grabbing Mark by the shoulder.

"What's up, man?"

"Mark, I need a favor."

His friend studied him. "Anything. Just name it."

"Your old lady friend from the D.O. Janine?"

"Janelle. The secretary. And it was *one* date, Luke."

"Whatever, listen. The new English teacher, Greta."

Mark blew his whistle and called for a water break then turned to Luke and crossed his arms. "Oh, you need a fairy godmother. Is that it?"

"No. But the school *does*."

"What do you mean?"

"They're dragging their feet with getting new hire contracts out, apparently. She seems to be courting another district. Up north."

"But school's already started. We've reported. She has a classroom. Rosters. She can't just leave." Scorn filled his face.

Luke shrugged. Mark was right. What kind of a person just quit like that? Was he blinded by... a crush?

Regardless of that, he still cared about keeping a good teacher around, and he didn't blame her if she was a little anxious about not signing on the dotted line. "Without a contract, she *can* leave."

"Then it wasn't meant to be, bud," Mark replied, laying into his whistle and barking off a new set of commands.

Chapter 19—Greta

Greta left for home. Or, rather, *Maggie's* home. With each passing day, Hickory Grove *was* feeling more and more like the place she belonged, that was true. Plus, the first day of teaching trainings went better than could be expected. Of course, the innkeeper's house was simply adorable. And affordable. And the Inn was so modest and low-key that she could totally manage any overnight duties, especially for the price and location. Then there was Luke. Greta had never in her life believed in fast love. She was not one to give into lust. Crushes came and went.

But *Luke*. Ugh. He was perfect.

It scared her.

What scared her even worse? Starting a job without a sure-fire paycheck. Greta could handle a rowdy class. She could handle subbing. She couldn't handle no pay. It was the number-one driving force in her life at the present.

Stories like this had circulated amongst some of her colleagues in the past. Horror stories about not receiving a teaching contract until a week or two into the school year. It seemed wild, but school officials were human, too. And in a rural area? It happened. From her acquaintances' experiences, no one ever ultimately dropped the ball. But certainly, there had to be situations where something fell through. The references were poor, and the district backed out. Or vice versa. But Greta liked the principal and her new co-workers. She was enchanted by her classroom, so familiar it nearly brought her to her knees with nostalgia. The kids would be sweet and scruffy and the perfect mix of work ethic and small-town manners, even when they lacked the wisdom or worldliness of those students who had the luxury of growing up in bigger cities with better access to more resources.

What would her mother say? Find what makes you happy... and do it? How could that apply in Greta's current situation. It simply didn't. She'd need faith. More than a mustard seed of the stuff, to follow her heart.

She glanced at the clock on her dash. Gretchen would be at Mally's by then, for her afternoon shift. Poor thing. Talk about someone unable to follow her heart. She worked like a horse and followed someone else's dreams. When was Gretchen going to find the guts to tell her mom she didn't want to be a hairdresser? When it was too late?

Greta stored the conversation for the future, promising herself she'd shake some sense into the girl.

Rhett was the next best person to talk to about Chicago and H.G.M.S. and the Inn. He was just aloof enough to offer her an objective stance. And he wouldn't let something like a co-worker crush cloud his judgment. He was bigger than that.

***

"Are you *crazy*, Greta Houston? What in the world has gotten *into* you? You can't just leave. You're at the Middle School now! You made a commitment. To the school. This town. To *us*!"

Rhett's rage was blinding. He paced the barn in front of Greta like an angry father.

Taken aback, Greta fumbled over her words, her patience for the situation growing thin. Her patience for herself snapped entirely. "It was just an *idea*, Rhett. Geez. Calm down. You sound like Dad."

"Good, because you need someone to smack some sense into you. You've got it perfect. You've got a job and you've got a place to stay." He waved his hand about the barn space. "And you could have that house on Overlook if you want it. Why would you even entertain the thought of jumping ship and leaving. Who cares if Chicago Public Schools called you? Who cares?" He spat his words like poison.

Greta's face flushed with heat. "Mom would have told me to do what makes me happy, you know." Small and quiet were her words as she crossed her arms and narrowed her gaze on her older brother.

"You're dragging Mom into this?" His face opened in mock surprise. "Okay, I can work with that. You're saying Mom would want you to be happy. And you're implying that leaving here after you already started... you think that would make you happy? Or is it a burning desire to live in Chicago? Or what, Greta, is it that running away makes you happy?" He shook his head, as a chill coursed up Greta's spine. Rhett continued, "Let me tell you something, Greta. You couldn't see it, because you were too busy chasing perfection, but Mom didn't leave Hickory Grove because she wanted something better. She didn't want to go back to Philly because of so-called opportunity. Philly wasn't her happiness. She went back for her parents. Her *family*. You and I left, so she did, too."

His claim stunned her. Their mom was not sentimental. She didn't attach meaning to things or places. That was a hard truth.

But much like Greta, she attached great meaning to her family. She needed them near. "She was sad we left? But we had to leave, Rhett. For college. And jobs."

"For opportunities, right?" he agreed. "Greta, whatever you're searching for—this 'happiness' thing... don't you think you've *found* it?"

She set her jaw, tears stinging the corners of her eyes. This was exactly why she wasn't sure she could hack it in Hickory Grove. She was under the microscope. Held accountable. Building a perfect life could never be possible when other people were on your back about how you lived your life.

Or did she have it all wrong?

Had Greta been searching for happiness since her mom died?

Or running from it?

Maggie's kitchen was something out of *Steel Magnolias*. Three women were perched in various chairs, sipping sweet tea as Maggie worked on someone's head at the sink. Greta smiled at the scene.

"Becky, will you take this?" Maggie asked her best friend, handing over a balled-up foil. Becky Linden had returned to Hickory Grove just the fall before. Her son, Theo, was Gretchen's boyfriend. She'd opened a bookshop in the old schoolhouse near the sold-off Houston property. She wasn't around much, and even Maggie mainly saw her at the shop, where Maggie pitched in on a regular basis. Greta had learned all this from Gretchen, who had suffered some jealousy from the revived friendship. Things were better now, though, especially since Becky's free time got sucked up with her own significant other, Zack Durbin, a lawyer in town.

Becky grabbed the wadded aluminum and tossed it in the trash. At the table, Gretchen was cutting new squares and neatly stacking them. Miss Fern sat at the table, shucking corn.

"Mind if I help?" Greta asked, taking a seat near Fern.

"Speak of the devil," Maggie drawled from the sink, lifting an eyebrow at Greta as she massaged acerbic shampoo into the stranger's head.

Paling at the accusation, Greta lowered herself slowly into the seat and locked eyes with Gretchen, who offered a sympathetic expression. What had they been talking about and with whom? Greta didn't mind so much if Maggie and Gretchen had words behind her back. And Fern seemed sweet enough. Becky, she didn't know. And the stranger, well, Greta began to reconsider her offer.

"Honey, you are the star of this conversation," Becky said, smiling sweetly.

"What are you all talking about?" Greta asked, flicking another look at Gretchen, who shrugged and resumed her foil-organizing. "And what's all this corn for?" she added, grabbing a cob and getting to work pulling back the green husk.

"Ladies Auxiliary asked me to coordinate food for this coming Fry-day. It'll be our biggest yet. The boys have a scrimmage right after. The whole town will be there, and the enemy's been invited, too."

"I told her to wait until Friday to get started. Or Thursday at least. People want fresh food, but Fern is too dead set on being ready ahead of time. It's like she's not from here or something."

Maggie winked at Greta and rinsed the stranger's head.

"I meant when you said speak of the devil." Greta set the newly naked corn cob in Fern's pile and reached for another, averting her gaze now.

"Well," Maggie answered, "Rumor has it you don't want to rent the Inn."

Greta let out a breath. At least Rhett hadn't given away her other secret. That she might blaze out of town in pursuit of something better. She wasn't going to anymore, so that little tidbit could die right now.

"Well, I might. I just need to settle into my new job a little. You know?"

Gretchen kept her gaze on the corn in her hands. Greta frowned. "I probably will, though. Who told you? Luke?"

Fern gave her a look as if to say *wake up and smell the pie*, and Greta smiled. "Oh, right. You probably talked to..."

Just then, Maggie secured a little towel around her customer's head, and the woman stood up and whipped around.

Liesel.

Greta wanted to sink into the farmhouse floor right then and there.

"Hi, Miss Liesel."

"Greta, dear, you don't have to rent that place. We weren't speaking ill of you. I understand. It's a big deal to move."

The others kept quiet as Liesel moved to the table and took the last remaining seat. She covered Greta's hand with hers. The woman's neat red manicure paired perfectly with her crimson lipstick. Penciled eyebrows arched over pale blue eyes, and for a moment, Greta wondered how the woman could be a spinster. She was drop-dead beautiful, articulate. Severe, sure. Without all the makeup and attention to her appearance, she'd make a great nun, Greta suspected.

"What will you do if I don't?"

Greta, in fact, wanted nothing more than to have a little place of her own. And the house on Overlook could be perfect. But the barn had become perfect, too. Perfect outside of Gretchen's displeasure and the fact that it would never really belong to her.

Then again, neither would the innkeeper's house. Greta wanted something that could belong to her, even if it wasn't hers.

"We'll figure it out, Greta. One of our relatives might be interested in purchasing the place, though Luke won't stand for it. Maybe we won't need to, though."

"Not if you let us help you fix up that sweet little Inn," Maggie trilled from the sink, where she was tidying up her tinctures.

"What?" Greta asked, more confused than ever.

"Listen, honey. If Luke and I are going to keep that place alive, it needs a makeover. I've come to accept it with the help of Fern and company here." She waved a hand around. "Someone to be on call at night, well, Luke and I can handle that for the time being. If we can bring more attention to the place, more draw, more guests... then people will be knocking down the door to live in that house."

"That's what I said." Maggie clicked her tongue and returned to Liesel's hair, unfolding it from the towel to reveal bright blonde tresses.

"I knew you could pull it off," Fern marveled. "Blonde is the way to go."

"Oh, please," Gretchen cut in, finally smiling a little. "Brunettes are taken more seriously."

"Classic Gretchen," Maggie replied, laughing. She turned her attention to Greta. "We're going to all help fix up the Hickory Grove Inn. Do you want to help? Or are you too busy juggling your new job and your little crush?"

At that, Greta turned beet red.

This was *not* what she wanted. Not to be treated like some teenager with a thing for a teacher. Indignant, she shook her head. What she said next, fell out of her mouth even though it wasn't the whole truth. Not after her lecture from Rhett. Not after her come-to-Jesus about the search for happiness. Greta wasn't going anywhere. Still, she said it to distract them. After all, Greta didn't want Liesel to think of her as some doe-eyed groupie, looking to shack up in the Inn just to be near the woman's precious nephew. "I got another job offer, actually."

Maggie's jaw nearly hit the ground. A comb fell from her hand, clattering to the floor dramatically.

"Why?" Gretchen asked, her eyes wide.

Greta didn't expect her to react like that. Gretchen should be happy to learn there was a chance her precious barn might free up.

Discomfort turned to anxiety in Greta's stomach, so she blurted it out. The whole story. She began with how she'd been applying *everywhere* but *no* school district was hiring, and if they were, they weren't hiring someone with a hodgepodge track record and a broken engagement, probably. She confessed her infatuation with Luke, and how it was painfully uncomfortable to know she'd have to see him every day. What if he didn't return her sentiments? What if he did and it soured?

She explained her mother's adage and how Rhett slapped some sense into her. Lastly, she told them about the case of the missing teaching contract, and how it felt like a sign.

"A sign!" Fern hollered. "It's a sign that our local school district can't get it together."

"Greta," Becky cut in. She'd kept her distance, being less familiar to Greta. Her voice was low as she went on. "Do you really want to stay at the middle school? Do you want to stay in Hickory Grove?"

Greta studied her, blinking. If anyone in the room knew her predicament, it was Becky. She'd been gone for decades, returning to make a beautiful life in the town she'd left behind for brighter horizons.

The idea that you can't really go home again had nagged at the back of Greta's mind. Seeing Becky, though, brought that other, secondary fear to light. Maybe it wasn't true. Maybe you could.

Maybe Greta could stop running and start staying. "Yes," she whispered to Becky.

"Then we can find out about that niggly little contract right now."

"Brilliant," Maggie added, her eyes flashing.

Greta watched as Becky tugged her phone from her purse and put a call in.

"No, no, no," Greta hissed across the room, her arm outstretched to prevent the woman from humiliating her by calling the school.

Gretchen grabbed Greta's arm midair and read her mind. "Shh, don't worry. She's not calling the school."

"Who's she calling, then?"

Fern answered, "Her boyfriend, Zack. He's the lawyer for the school district. He has an office there."

Greta's eyes grew wide. She waited. They all waited, watching and listening as Becky navigated Zack over the phone.

"It is?" Becky said after some pause. "You're positive?"

Giddy now, Greta looked at Fern, whispering, "Is that even allowed?"

Becky ended the call before Fern could answer, and Greta looked at her. "Are you sure he can do that?"

"He didn't do anything," Becky replied. "He was leaving his office and happened to see a document on the printer."

Her heart beat faster. A grin spread across Greta's mouth.

Maggie cackled.

Greta let out a breath. "So, they *do* want me to teach there? They didn't find a reason to wiggle out of it?" Her insecurities flooded out, but she let them, finding relief in the chance to vent. She could be herself, again. After a couple of years of trying to be perfect, of trying to find that perfect life that would erase her sadness, she could breathe.

"No one wants *you* to wiggle out of here," Maggie said, snipping the ends off of Liesel's hair. "Don't be silly!"

Liesel smiled. "Listen, Greta. You don't have to rent the Inn. Live where you want. But you just made yourself a group of girlfriends. And you *do* have to help us get ready for this darn fish fry."

Greta smiled, and the others laughed.

But Gretchen held up her hand. "Actually, she can live anywhere she wants *except* for my sewing barn."

"Sewing barn?" Maggie asked, scoffing. "Girl, you need a sewing *machine* first."

"I didn't know you liked to sew," Liesel commented lightly. "I'm a quilter, myself." As their banter wore on, Greta felt more at home than ever.

She excused herself to make a call, and by then, she knew she was making the right choice for once. The truly right choice. Greta glanced at the time on her phone before it began to ring. Just before five. She crossed her fingers that it wasn't too late.

A woman answered immediately, greeting her with a terse *hello*.

"Hi, this is Greta Houston. We spoke a little bit ago about my application?"

The woman's tone changed. "Greta, hello! Yes. So glad to hear back from you."

"Thank you," Greta went on, forcing herself to keep from grinning ear to ear. "I have my answer."

Chapter 20—Luke

After practice, Luke drove straight home, showered, and dove into bed, tossing and turning the whole night.

He woke up expecting to dread the workday. No doubt she wouldn't be there. How could he tolerate meetings and Power-Points and a soggy sandwich for lunch if he didn't have the new teacher to distract him? The potential tenant? The potential... *everything.*

Since practice the evening before, Luke had missed no fewer than five calls from Liesel. He'd ignored them all, knowing full-well that if it was an emergency she'd text or leave a message. But she hadn't. And he didn't care.

The Inn could fall into bankruptcy. Sudden depression threatened to descend on him. But it lifted a little by the time he showed up in the cafeteria. Mark held a plate piled high with eggs, two waffles drenched in syrup, and fresh cut fruit.

"A breakfast upgrade?" Luke asked, setting his clipboard down at the same seat he'd used the day before. The one next to Greta's, which stood empty.

Mark plopped his plate down and pointed a finger to the buffet. "The D.O. put it on. Elementary and high school are joining us today, so, you know how it is. They blow it out."

Luke had forgotten. Day two was a little different, with a whole-district meeting then smaller breakout sessions.

As if on cue, a rash of vaguely familiar faces flooded the doorway, converging on the buffet.

Luke got in line, trudging his way toward the only thing that could cure a wounded heart: downhome food.

Returning to the table, he found four new faces replacing the English department. He glanced at Mark who shrugged. "They said to sit with your kind."

"Our *kind*?" Luke laughed and shook hands with P.E. teachers from the high school and elementary school. The others shot the breeze until the conversation rounded to the football program. It snapped Luke out of his ongoing search for Greta. He tore his eyes away from one of the two tables where he'd spied Susan, one of the other English teachers, for a fleeting moment.

"Good season ahead," he agreed distractedly.

"You all going to the fish fry before the game?" Mark asked the other coaches.

They nodded.

"Can't. It'll be too close." Luke sipped on his coffee, burning the tip of his tongue and muttering a swear.

"Aw, come on. We can grab a plate and take off after, right?"

"Aren't the boys going?" one of the others asked.

Luke shrugged. "If they can get to the warm-up time." He hated his own attitude but felt compelled to be irritated.

Mrs. Cook's voice blasted on the microphone as she welcomed the other two faculties to the middle school. Then she gave the mic over to the superintendent, who launched into a familiar welcome-back speech.

Luke's eyes never stopped scanning, but the crowd was too thick. He'd have to stand up to search for her, and that would be ridiculous.

Then, the superintendent passed the microphone to the elementary principal, who started introducing her new hires for the year.

Suddenly hopeful again, Luke eased back in his chair.

With each name she called, a nervous head popped up, the person half-standing from their chair and waving a hand awkwardly at the recognition.

The elementary school's new hires totaled two.

After that, the superintendent invited Mrs. Cook to return, but she waved him off as she whispered together with Barb. Luke frowned when the high school principal took over, calling out the names of three more new people, two of them custodians.

Mrs. Cook, apparently, still was not ready, so the superintendent took the liberty of sharing his own new hires, one bus driver and a new technology assistant.

Luke thought his head was going to burst. His heart was going to burst. His leg bounced beneath the table, consuming some of his overwhelming energy.

At last, Mrs. Cook took the microphone again, twirling herself in front of the podium and flashing a broad smile. To Luke's knowledge, she had only one name to introduce. One person. Was she going to say the name he was longing to hear? Or would she say that there were no new hires. Would she say there *had* been a new hire, but she flaked out? Had she found a replacement for Greta in those few hours since he'd seen her last? Had Greta called the school, cancelled her promise, and left town? And maybe Mrs. Cook dragged someone off the street to join the team? To *make H.G.M.S. great!*?

"I'm so happy to introduce our newest team member," Mrs. Cook cheered into the microphone. "A big-city transplant, we convinced her to give little Hickory Grove a shot..."

Luke winced, squeezing his eyes shut, then opening them again to scan the crowd.

"Joining our English department this year is..."

Sweat broke out along his spine. His leg froze mid-bounce. Deafening silence filled the cafeteria as though every other person was also awaiting that moment.

"Miss Greta Houston!"

A spunky blonde head shot up beneath a slender arm. As she waved across the cafeteria, her eyes fell on Luke.

They stayed there after she sat down and the school leaders moved on to the next item of business. They stayed there for some moments, until at last, Greta and Luke smiled at each other.

A smile that could move mountains. Perform miracles. A smile that could end his football program if he were a lesser man.

But he wasn't. And at that moment, Luke Hart knew every aspect of his life was about to have just a little more meaning. That smile meant Luke was going to become a *better* man. A P.E. teacher who could inspire even the laziest student. A football coach who could win championships. A nephew who could help his aunt turn their shared investment into something to be proud of.

A grandson who would turn his mamaw's old house into a home. If not for Greta, then for himself. And for whoever would one day share that home.

Liesel may never be ready. But Luke was.

Chapter 21—Greta

The week was a blur. Between setting up her classroom and attending obligations, Greta barely caught her breath before the first day of school, which was Thursday.

Every opportunity to see or chat with Luke was stolen. Tuesday was a bust, as they were shuffled immediately into departmental meetings before she had to spend the afternoon in HR, filling out new hire paperwork and finding her way down to the county offices to have her certificate stamped.

Wednesday was classroom prep then home to get ready for back-to-school night, which lasted well past seven.

She had dawdled in the parking lot afterwards, hoping to catch a glimpse of him only to realize he was probably at football practice by then.

When they wound up at the same water fountain after first hour on Thursday, they exchanged a smile, and there it was. That feeling. Greta knew he shared it. They tried to make small talk over student heads, but the bell rang, sending them apart yet again.

Every single night, Greta thumbed her phone, going back and forth over whether to be the first to make a move.

Gretchen had shown up in the barn Thursday, after her shift. She didn't bring up the barn, but that didn't matter since Greta had made up her mind already. It was just a matter of sticking to the plan and seeing it through. There'd be no argument.

When Greta mentioned how she couldn't seem to connect with Luke, Gretchen had just shrugged. "Fry-day."

"What do you mean?" Greta asked.

"The fish fry. He works every single one. Just show up. Like last time, right?" The girl had grinned and winked, leaving Greta with another book in exchange for nothing. She was a sweetheart. Greta didn't deserve her friendship.

But the advice was solid.

Anyway, Greta was already helping out with the fish fry. Liesel and Fern roped her into joining the Ladies Auxiliary.

So, there she was on Friday. As soon as school had let out, she scrambled over to help set up. Once her tasks were done, Greta asked the others if she could slip away to freshen up before the festivities began.

They agreed easily, giggling behind her back as she all but darted to her car, scrambling home and back in a fresh sundress, with her hair in soft waves about her face. Pink lip gloss and strappy sandals. A summer tan and the boldness that came out of a week of wanting. Wanting to see him. Wanting to talk to him. Wanting, especially, to apologize to him. Set him straight. She was in town to stay, and he'd have to deal with it, and...

But he never showed up.

No one saw him, either. Greta checked. None of the football players she'd asked, as they rushed to get their plates, gobbled down a supper before heading into souped-up pickups and speeding off down the dirt lane and out towards the high school.

Not Fern or Maggie or Gretchen.

Liesel, however, assured Greta that he was at the game. Liesel argued that Greta's best bet was to go there, cheer the team on, then hang around after.

"I'm not a groupie," Greta declared. "Maybe he doesn't want to see me."

His aunt threw a sidelong look at Greta. "He *wants* to see you. He doesn't know how, sweetheart."

"What do you mean?"

Liesel sighed. "After college, which I'm sure was the wildest time of his life," she chuckled good naturedly, "once he settled down here, this town became his world. And the people in it. Football, school, Little Flock. He hasn't dated much. When you hinted that you weren't sticking around, you scared him off."

"For good?" Greta asked, horror clenching her chest, depriving her of a full breath.

"No," Liesel confirmed. "Listen, Greta. If you want to talk to my nephew, even just say hello, why not do it privately anyway? It'll give you a chance to explain everything."

"Privately?" Greta asked, dubious.

"You don't want to confront him in front of forty sweaty teenage boys. Or here, for that matter. This weekend, he's working the night shift."

"You mean at The—"

Liesel nodded, smiling.

***

After the football game, which Greta went to, all thirty-seven hours of it (or so, it felt), she vacillated briefly over Liesel's advice. She was fairly certain that Luke had glanced up at the bleachers once or twice. She thought he saw her. She even waved once, but he'd turned around by then.

When the team poured out of the locker room, Greta spied Luke smackdab in the middle, next to Mark, walking with a pep in his step, high on their victory.

One by one, the boys left. Tailgates shut and the parking lot cleared out. Mark and Luke stood at the edge of the parking lot. Greta sat in her car in the middle of a few other stragglers. Parents who were still waiting for their younger sons to finish up. Maggie drove past, pausing at the curb to collect Ky and Dakota, the dutiful water boys.

Eventually, there were too few cars, but Luke and Mark remained, waiting for the last of the athletes to be picked up. She couldn't sit there any longer. Her cover would be blown. He knew her car. Maybe he even knew she was waiting.

So, Greta left.

Chapter 22—Luke

Luke parked and hopped out, dog tired but happy. Even a scrimmage win was a W. Plus, he saw her. There in the stands, looking like a cheerleader who had aged with taste and class. The only thing missing was some sort of contact. A wave or a smile. Instead, she sat like a soldier, and each time he glanced up, her face was serious. Like she had a lot to think about.

Maybe she did.

There were just a couple of things on his checklist before bedtime, and he full-well intended to wrap things up and get home right away. He had morning practice.

Inside, Luke did a quick walk-through, locking the giftshop and securing the back door to the garden. He checked the till then went through the guest log, committing the names to memory and double checking his phone for any urgent questions or concerns.

In the coming weeks, there would be a full-blown reno, led by the Little Flock Ladies Auxiliary, Maggie Devereux, and Greta's own brother, Rhett. They'd all agreed to help spruce the place up and bring out its full potential. Luke felt both excited and nervous. Mostly nervous that Greta might involve herself, which could be awkward. For both of them.

That night, Stella had left an hour early to watch her son play in the scrimmage, and though Liesel offered to take over and wrap things up, he wanted to. He needed to.

Just as Luke was about to slap the book shut and call it a night, the front door cracked open.

Alarmed, he took a long step around the desk, one arm out. "Who's there?" he demanded, his voice gruff.

The door opened wider, and he repeated himself. "Who's *there*?"

Blonde hair appeared. "Me. It's me." Her sweet, small voice slipped around the door, and her face appeared beneath that pretty head of hair. He wanted to comb his fingers through it, tousle it.

"Greta?"

"I'm sorry. Am I bothering you?"

He grinned, dropping his arm and relaxing. "Of course not. What are you doing here?"

She smiled back, mischievous. "I saw the sign."

"What sign?" he scratched his head then crossed his arms over his chest, uncertain.

"Vacancy. You have a room for rent?"

Studying her, Luke answered with a question. "Did poor Gretchen finally kick you out of her sewing house or whatever she calls it?"

Greta mock-frowned. "How did you know about that little drama?"

"She complained to me at Mally's. Before I even met you. Actually, it was the first day I saw you there. Coming in. She'd told Mark and me about how someone was moving into her sewing house."

"It's a barn, for your information," Greta corrected him. "But I'm moving now. She didn't have to kick me out."

"What, you're going back to Chicago? Or maybe Indianapolis? Does your *fiancé* want to reunite?" He couldn't help it. A shadow crossed his face, and all the little things he knew about her and didn't know started to spread through his mind, surfacing on his tongue like little daggers. Ammunition in the mini war between them. The one that played out over her Chicago phone call. Over her unavailability. He wasn't angry with Greta. He wasn't. But he was on guard.

"And how did you know about *that*?" Now she frowned more seriously.

He winced. "I'm sorry. Small town, remember? Word gets around."

"He's old news, I can assure you of that."

Luke nodded. He believed her. "I'd love to know more about it. Er, I mean... I'd love to know more about *you*, you know."

A skeptical expression crossed her face. "You *would*?"

"It wasn't obvious?"

Greta blinked, smiled, and nodded. "Well, same here." Biting her lip, she twisted slowly, her eyes dancing around the place.

"Is that why you came?" he asked.

She shrugged. "Yes and no. I really am interested in your vacancy."

"You want a room in here? With a double bed and a Norman Rockwell hanging on the wall?" He chuckled. "Surely you can do better. Even if it's a sewing house."

"Barn," she corrected again. He held up his hands in apology, but she went on. "Actually, Luke. I'm interested in your mamaw's house. If, that is, it's still available?"

He felt the wind knock out of him. Swallowing, he formed a response. "It might not be."

Her face fell. "Oh." A wrinkle knit her brows together.

"Actually," Luke answered, licking his lips and rerouting. "What I mean is… it might not be available *long-term*." He was backpedaling on his own decision, but he had to. Here she was, the girl of his dreams, asking if she could do exactly what he had wanted her to do all along. How could he say no? Still, he had to stick to something. "I'm selling my house."

"You're moving into the house? Your mamaw's house?" Her expression softened, but sadness dwelt behind her eyes.

"Yes. Liesel and I discussed it. Not yet, but once I can sell my place. I was thinking next summer. I'll have more time then, and—"

Out of the clear blue, Greta took a step to him, put her hand on his chest and rose up on her toes.

And kissed him.

Luke closed his eyes and dropped his hands to her waist, pulling her into him and parting his lips. It remained chaste. Soft.

When he opened his eyes, she was staring up at him. "I'm sorry," Greta whispered.

He furrowed his brow, his hands still on her waist. "For what?"

"For being indecisive. For suggesting I was going to leave." She closed her eyes and paused a beat before opening them again.

"You don't have to apologize, Greta. I know it's hard to… I know you were going through something now. I get it."

The corners of her mouth pricked up. "I'm also sorry I didn't say yes before."

"To what?" he replied.

"To being your tenant." She shrugged. "I am moving from the barn. Somewhere. It belongs to Gretchen. And I belong somewhere that's my own, too. If not here," she waved an arm, pulling away from his grip, "then I can stay at Rhett's house. He's almost done with it, and he'll have a spare room. From there, my back-up plan is to rent from him. Maybe I could even buy. He has a few properties in Louisville you know, and—"

This time, Luke lifted a finger to her mouth, quieting her rambling. "Greta," he said. "If you want to live in Mamaw's house, it's all yours."

He ducked his head and pressed his mouth to hers again. It was soon, but it was right. She kissed him back, and when they parted, her arms climbed up his shoulders, tugging him into a deep hug. "Thank you."

Then, Greta dropped back to her heels, pushing away. "Just for the school year. Okay? After that, I'll buy my own place. Maybe I'll buy yours!" She laughed then flashed a broad smile at him.

"Maybe. Maybe not," he answered, lifting an eyebrow.

"What do you mean?"

Luke cupped her face in his hands, suddenly so comfortable with the beautiful stranger who stood before him. The Hickory Grove local. The schoolteacher all of his students were already raving about. The heartbroken woman who'd lost her mother and was trying... trying *so* hard to make a life for herself. And he kissed her again before murmuring, at last, "You never know what might happen in a year."

***

Epilogue

One year later.

"Welcome to The Hickory Grove Inn!" Greta flashed a bright smile to her new guests. A freshly married couple who opted for an RV trip across America for their honeymoon. Greta's kind of people. "You must be the Hennings?"

After passing an old-fashioned brass key to the wife, Greta glanced at the grandfather clock. It was one of many of Mamaw Hart's personal effects which she had convinced Liesel and Luke to dust off and bring up from the basement. With careful selection of heirlooms and a few new touches, The Hickory Grove Inn had turned from a dark and barren wood lodging to the charming bed-and-breakfast the Harts had likely envisioned years back. With Liesel's oversight and blessings, heavy velvet curtains were exchanged for lace. Cream-colored doilies sat atop refurbished dressers. Tiffany lamps and natural light flooded the space, brightening it and bringing it back to life.

"It's just after seven, which means you're right on time to enjoy our evening sherry."

"Sherry?" the husband asked, cocking his head to Greta then his wife for an explanation. When the latter came up empty, Greta gushed out a bubbly response.

"That's right. In Hickory Grove, no one goes to bed without a little something to wet the whistle. We abide by Mamaw Hart's late tradition. A sherry a day keeps the doctor away! After you get settled in upstairs, then you can join the other guests and our evening hostess for a glass of the good stuff. Just here," she paused along their brief tour of the first floor, "in the parlor."

Gretchen waved merrily from the wet bar where she stood arranging decanters and heavy crystal glasses. Greta insisted Gretchen work *less*, but the determined girl begged to help out at the Inn. It was her escape. A fresh hobby and something to fill her evenings when her boyfriend was away at college.

They paused at the parlor which was once the employee break room. Greta knew it had to reclaim its original purpose when Stella revealed she'd never used it once. There was no reason not to open the first floor and create a homey area apart from the dining room. The evening sherry and the midmorning and afternoon snacks were now offered there, in the parlor, instead of the dining room, which was reserved only for breakfast, brunch, and special events. Yes, Greta had seen to it that her new family business was more than an evening respite. It now rivaled the river boat casino for nearly all local events, so long as the coordinating clients were looking for southern charm and quaint delight. With the rear garden finally growing lush and colorful, they even had an outdoor venue. Another project Liesel was happy for Greta to take on. It seemed that the Hart matriarch was only too pleased to have her nephew's wife take a fervent interest in carrying on family traditions. And creating new ones.

Once Greta and the newlyweds returned to the staircase, she gestured up to the second floor. "Take a left on the landing, third door on your right." It had been two weeks since she stopped climbing the stairs every time someone checked in. Luke was too worried she might take a fall.

The bell that hung above the front door clanged to life, and her husband entered, clad in athletic shorts and a white tee, his summer uniform. His everyday uniform, in truth.

The newlyweds ascended the staircase, murmuring compliments within earshot. Greta returned to finish checking them in as Luke strode to the desk, leaning overtop of it and pressing his lips to her cheek.

"How was practice?" Greta asked, flushing at his chaste kiss and glowing with happiness to see him.

"Good, good. Lookin' like another championship year. Did you talk to Mrs. Cook yet?"

Greta nodded, smiling. "The substitute agreed to take it on long term. I'm set for the school year."

Luke grinned and pushed off of the desk, holding his hand out once Greta locked the till and rounded towards him.

She rested her other hand on top of her growing belly, allowing Luke to guide her through the front door and over to their home, the innkeeper's-quarters-turned-family-house.

Twinkling stars filled the milky night sky, lighting their path as Luke guided his pregnant wife up to the front porch and swept her inside, out of the warm evening air.

When it came time for them to move in, just six months before, the week after their wedding, Greta insisted on restoring rather than renovating the old family place. Luke and Liesel were thrilled over this, but Greta had always sensed Liesel felt a little sad about the whole thing.

Sad in general, perhaps.

Liesel had even confessed as much during one of the Ladies Auxiliary meetings, which compelled Greta to start working on the problem, adding yet another thing to her growing to-do list. She wouldn't have it any other way. For Greta, busy was good. Busy was *great*.

Projects brought joy to her. Once she had moved into the house next to the Inn and started the school year at H.G.M.S., it occurred to Greta that searching for happiness outside of herself had never been the answer. True happiness had always been there, where she was born and raised, in the place where her mother had laid down roots. The place Greta was so certain her mother wanted to give up.

But as soon as Luke had proposed marriage, happiness hit Greta like a tidal wave, consuming her and drowning her in the stuff. It was then that Greta fully knew the meaning of her mother's advice. *Find what makes you happy and do it.* The *find* part was never about the search.

It was about the acceptance. The contentedness. The bird in the hand, even.

Still, as if starting a new teaching job and planning a wedding and restoring an old house weren't enough, Greta realized something more. Something else that was missing from her life. Not romance, which she had in abundance—an old-fashioned courtship with Luke Hart was the most romantic thing she'd ever experience. It wasn't family that she was missing, either. Living close to her brother was like a revival of her childhood. Summer mornings in Maggie's kitchen cemented Greta in a new sisterhood, too. Though they didn't quite replace her bond with her mother, they helped to fill it.

Of course, the kitchen with its perm fumes and the errant child running through with a squawking chicken was not ideal for what Greta pinned down as the missing ingredient in her perfect life.

They needed a new locale. A place to convene either as the Ladies Auxiliary or simply as a group of girlfriends.

Little did Greta and her new friends realize, but such a space was sitting right beneath their noses.

In the place that had touched Greta's life. And Gretchen's. Maggie's too. And Liesel's once she helped Gretchen get started, learning to work the antique sewing machine. Fern's when she donated an entire closetful of fabric. And Becky's when they discovered in there a whole stash of ancient seamstress books, leftover from Maggie's ancestors.

So, Greta led the women in establishing a place for Liesel to teach Gretchen about sewing. A place for friends to meet. A place to sip sweet tea and plan weddings and do all the things that girlfriends liked to do. A place that could be a patchwork blanket, unifying the hodgepodge group of women like a cozy wrap.

It was originally an old barn. But they came to call it the Quilting House.

***

Other Titles by Elizabeth Bromke

About the Author

Elizabeth Bromke is the author of the Maplewood series, the Hickory Grove series, and the Birch Harbor series. Each set of stories incorporates family, friends, and love.

Elizabeth lives in the mountains of Arizona, where she enjoys reading, writing, and spending time with her family.

Learn more about the author by visiting elizabeth-bromke.com today.

Made in the USA
Middletown, DE
02 November 2023

41813347R00109